PART ONE OF JOHN SAUL'S CHILLING SERIAL TALE

The time is the present. The place is the New Hampshire town of Blackstone, a peaceful picture postcard village with a shattering, painful past. For here, high on North Hill stands the old Blackstone Asylum, once the home of the deranged, the unmanageable, and the merely inconvenient. Long abandoned, the building is scheduled for demolition. Yet something halts those plans—and a terrible evil, once locked within its formidable stone walls, lurches into the night. Its horrifying power takes on many forms: appearing as seemingly harmless gifts, mysteriously delivered to various members of the Blackstone community. The first is a beautiful antique doll. Perfect for a young girl—and oh so deadly. . . .

THE BLACKSTONE CHRONICLES
AN EYE FOR AN EYE: THE DOLL

By John Saul:
SUFFER THE CHILDREN
PUNISH THE SINNERS
CRY FOR THE STRANGERS
COMES THE BLIND FURY
WHEN THE WIND BLOWS
THE GOD PROJECT
NATHANIEL
BRAINCHILD
HELLFIRE
THE UNWANTED
THE UNLOVED
CREATURE
SECOND CHILD
SLEEPWALK
DARKNESS
SHADOWS
GUARDIAN*
THE HOMING*
BLACK LIGHTNING*
THE BLACKSTONE CHRONICLES, Part 1
    AN EYE FOR AN EYE: THE DOLL*

*Published by Fawcett Books

THE BLACKSTONE CHRONICLES

PART 1
AN EYE FOR AN EYE: THE DOLL

John Saul

FAWCETT CREST • NEW YORK

A Fawcett Crest Book
Published by Ballantine Books
Copyright © 1997 by John Saul

All rights reserved under International and Pan-American Copyright Conventions. Published in the United States by Ballantine Books, a division of Random House, Inc., New York, and simultaneously in Canada by Random House of Canada Limited, Toronto.

http://www.randomhouse.com

Library of Congress Catalog Card Number: 96-90779

ISBN 0-449-22781-2

Manufactured in the United States of America

First Edition: February 1997

10 9 8 7 6 5 4 3 2 1

For Linda Grey, with
love and gratitude

Dear Reader,

Over the past twenty years, it has been my pleasure to entertain you with books relating tales of terror and mayhem. But, as I'm sure you've suspected, there are at least as many stories I haven't yet told, for the very simple reason that they have never fit comfortably into the publishing form we call "the novel."

Now, thanks to Stephen King and his groundbreaking serial novel, *The Green Mile*, a newly revitalized form of publication has become available to us all. The form of the serial is far from new—its history stretches from Dickens's serialized novels in the 1850s and '60s through the Saturday afternoon adventures that my generation enjoyed in movie theaters. But serial novels haven't appeared since my grandfather's day—until *The Green Mile*.

So it was with mounting excitement that I watched as subsequent installments of King's tale proved that the form is as fresh today as it was when Dickens employed it. For ever since I wrote my first novel, *Suffer the Children*, I have been living with the fictional town of Blackstone in my head. I clearly see the village in New Hampshire, right down the road from Port Arbello; its shady tree-lined streets, its even more shadowy history.

Its characters are vivid to me. (In fact, over the years, some characters from my other novels have moved to Blackstone, as you shall see.) Their secrets, their sins, and the sins of their fathers seem so real they are more like memories than inventions.

There are several leading families in my imaginary Blackstone—the Connallys, the Beckers, the McGuires, the Hartwicks. All have a part to play as the drama unfolds. Over the generations their lives have intertwined: births, marriages, deaths, business dealings, rivalries, hardships, and occasional triumphs (all the stuff of our lives, in other words) have created among them the connections—and separations—shared by these prominent citizens of my little town. Above all, one person, one series of shocking and secret circumstances, has bound them together. But how could I explain those relationships, those events—and the catalyst that set in motion the evil that now shadows their lives? What was the best way to tell these separate stories, each of them linked to long-hidden moments in the past, each of them linked to each other, each of them linked to a powerful force that is about to make its insidious presence known?

It seemed to me that this "new" form, the novel conceived in parts, or installments, provided the answer, and *The Blackstone Chronicles* finally began to take place for me on the printed page, as did the objects—artifacts of evil, if you will—that symbolized for me each of the stories I wanted to tell. *The Doll* is the first of these, and it arrives on the doorstep of the McGuire family in Part One. Who sent this gift to Elizabeth and Bill McGuire—and why—I leave you to discover. But I warn you that you won't know the full story until the very end, some months from now! In the meantime, several more presents from the past will have made their way to various carefully selected denizens of Blackstone. And I hope that as you finish the last page of each part another piece of the puzzle will have been revealed—and that you will experience the delicious thrill of anticipating the next installment. And as you finish each volume of *The Blackstone Chronicles*, perhaps you will let your imagination conjure up the terrors that might await in future installments.

So, without further ado, I offer you *An Eye for an Eye: The Doll*, the first of the half dozen gifts I've prepared for you this year.

I hope you enjoy them as much as I've enjoyed wrapping them.

—JOHN SAUL
October 10, 1996

The Beginning

*T*he old Seth Thomas Regulator began to chime the hour. Oliver Metcalf kept typing only long enough to finish the sentence before abandoning the editorial he was composing to gaze thoughtfully at the wood-cased clock that had hung on the wall of the *Blackstone Chronicle*'s one-room office for far more years than Oliver himself could remember. It was the clock that first fascinated him when his uncle brought him here more than forty years ago and taught him how to tell time, and the clock still fascinated him, with its rhythmic ticking, and because it kept time so perfectly that it had to be adjusted by no more than a single minute every year.

Now, after marking the thousands of hours of his life with its soft chime, it was reminding Oliver that the hour had come for him to perform his part in an event that would take place only once.

Today, the town of Blackstone was going to take the first, significant step in the destruction of part of its history.

Oliver Metcalf, as editor and publisher of the town's weekly newspaper, had been asked to make a speech. He'd made preparatory notes for several days but still had no idea precisely what he would say when the moment finally arrived for him to stand at the podium, the great stone structure rising behind him, and face his fellow townsmen. As he picked up the sheaf of notes and tucked it into the inside pocket of his tweed jacket, he

1

wondered if inspiration would strike him when at last he had to speak, or whether he would stare speechlessly out at the gathered crowd as they gazed, waiting, at him.

Questions would be in their minds.

Questions that no one had spoken aloud for years.

Questions to which he had no answers.

He locked the office door behind him and stepped out onto the sidewalk. Crossing the street to cut through the town square, he considered turning back, skipping the ceremony entirely and instead finishing the editorial upon which he'd been working all morning. It was, after all, exactly the kind of day that was meant for staying indoors. The sky was slate gray, and the previous night's wind had stripped the last of the leaves from the great trees that had spread a protective canopy above the town from spring through fall. In early spring, when the enormous oaks and maples first began to bud, the canopy was the palest of greens. But as summer progressed, the foliage matured and thickened, darkening to a deep green that shaded Blackstone from August's hot glare and sheltered it from the rain squalls that swept through on their way toward the Atlantic seacoast several miles to the east. Over the last few weeks, abundant green had given way to the splendor of fall, and for a while the village had gloried in autumn's shimmering golden, red, and russet tones. Now the ground was littered with leaves, already a dead-looking brown, already beginning the slow process of decay that would return them to the soil from which they'd originally sprung.

Oliver Metcalf started toward the top of the hill where most of the townspeople would soon be gathered. Snow had not yet fallen, but a sodden, chill rain had accompanied last night's wind. It seemed to Oliver that a damp, freezing winter was about to descend. The gray light of the day seemed perfectly to reflect his own bleak mood. The trees, with their huge, naked limbs, raised their skeletal branches grotesquely toward the sky, as if seeking to ward off the lowering clouds with fleshless, twisted fingers. Ducking his head against the ominous morning, Oliver walked quickly through the streets, nodding distractedly to the people who spoke to him, meanwhile trying to focus his mind on what he would say to the crowd that would soon be gathered around the best-known building in town.

The Blackstone Asylum.

Throughout Oliver's life—throughout the lives of everyone in Blackstone—the massive building, constructed of stones dug from the fields surrounding the village, had loomed at the top of the town's highest hill. Its long-shuttered windows gazed out over the town not as if it were abandoned, but rather as though it were sleeping.

Sleeping, and waiting someday to awaken.

A chill passed through Oliver as the thought crossed his mind, but he quickly shook it off. No, it would never happen.

Today, the destruction of the Blackstone Asylum would commence.

A wrecking ball would swing, hurling its weight against those heavy gray stones, and after dominating the town for a full century, the building would finally be torn apart, its stone walls demolished, its turrets fallen, its green copper roof sold off for scrap.

As Oliver stepped through the ornate wrought-iron gates that pierced the fence surrounding the Asylum's entire ten acres, and started up the wide, curving driveway leading to its front door, an arm fell across his shoulders and he heard his uncle's familiar voice.

"Quite a day, wouldn't you say, Oliver?" Harvey Connally said, his booming, hearty voice belying his eighty-three years.

Oliver's gaze followed his uncle's, fixing on the brooding building, and he wondered what was going through the old man's mind. No point in asking; for despite their closeness, he'd always found his uncle far more comfortable discussing ideas than emotions.

"If you talk about emotions, you have to talk about people," Harvey had told him back when he was only ten or eleven years old, and home from boarding school for Christmas. "And talking about people is gossip. I don't gossip, and you shouldn't either." The words had clearly signaled Oliver that there were many things his uncle did not want to discuss.

Still, as the old man gazed up at the building that had risen on North Hill only a few years before his birth, Oliver couldn't help trying one last time.

"Your father built it, Uncle Harvey," he said softly. "Aren't you just a little sorry to see it go?"

His uncle's grip tightened on his shoulder. "No, I'm not," Harvey Connally replied, his voice grating as he spoke the words. "And neither should you be. Good riddance to it, is what I say, and we should all forget everything that ever happened there."

His hand fell from Oliver's shoulder.

"Everything," he said again.

Half an hour later Oliver stood at the podium that had been erected in front of the Asylum's imposing portico, his eyes surveying the crowd. Nearly everyone had come. The president of the bank was there, as was the contractor whose company would demolish most of the old Asylum, keeping only the facade. The plan was to replace the interior with a complex of shops and restaurants that promised to bring a prosperity to Blackstone that no one had known since the years when the institution itself had provided the economic basis for the town's livelihood. Everyone who was involved in the project was there, but there were others as well, people whose parents and grandparents, even great-grandparents, had once worked within the stone walls behind him. Now they hoped that the new structure might provide their children and grandchildren with jobs.

Beyond the assemblage, just inside the gate, Oliver could see the small stone house that had been deeded to the last superintendent of the Asylum, upon the occasion of his marriage to the daughter of the chairman of the Asylum's board of directors.

When the Blackstone Asylum had finally been abandoned and its last superintendent had died, that house, too, stood empty for several years. Then the young man who had inherited it, having graduated from college, returned to Blackstone and moved back into that house, the house in which he'd been born.

Oliver Metcalf had come home.

He hadn't expected to sleep at all on that first night, but to his surprise, the two-story stone cottage seemed to welcome him back, and he'd immediately felt as if he was home. The ghosts he'd expected had not appeared, and within a few years he almost forgot he'd ever lived anywhere else. But in all the years since then, living in the shadow of the Asylum his father had once run, Oliver had not once set foot inside the building.

He'd told himself he had no need to.

Deep in his heart, he'd known he couldn't.

Something inside its walls—something unknowable— terrified him.

Now, as the crowd fell into an expectant silence, Oliver adjusted the microphone and began to speak.

"Today marks a new beginning in the history of Blackstone. For nearly a century, a single structure has affected every family—every individual—in our town. Today, we begin the process of tearing that structure down. This signifies not only the end of one era, but the beginning of another. The process of replacing the old Blackstone Asylum with the new Blackstone Center will not be simple. Indeed, when the new building is finally completed, its facade will look much as the Asylum looks today; constructed of the same stones that have stood on this site for nearly a hundred years, it will look familiar to all of us, but at the same time, all of it will be different. . . ."

For half an hour Oliver continued speaking, his thoughts organizing themselves as he spoke in the same simple, orderly prose that flowed from him when he sat at his computer, composing a feature or an editorial for the newspaper. Then, as the bell in the Congregational church downtown began to strike the hour of noon, he turned to Bill McGuire, the contractor who would oversee the demolition of the old building and construction of the new complex of shops and restaurants as well.

Nodding, Oliver stepped away from the podium, walked down the steps to join the crowd, and turned to face the building as the great lead wrecking ball swung for the first time toward the century-old edifice.

As the last chime of the church bell faded away, the ball punched through the west wall of the building. A sigh that sounded like a moaning wind passed through the crowd as it watched half a hundred fieldstones tumble to the ground, leaving a gaping hole in a wall that had stood solid through ten decades.

Oliver, though, heard nothing of the sigh, for as the ball smashed through the wall, a blinding flash of pain shot through his head.

Through the pain, a fleeting vision appeared . . .

A man walks up the steps toward the huge double doors of the Asylum. In his hand he holds the hand of a child.

The child is crying.

The man ignores the child's cries.

As man and boy approach the great oaken doors, they swing open.

Man and boy pass through.

The enormous doors swing closed again.

Prologue

The previous day's clouds had long since swept out to sea, and a full moon stood high in the sky. Atop North Hill the Asylum was silhouetted against a sky sparkling with the glitter of millions of stars while the night itself seemed infused with a silvery glow.

No one, though, was awake to see it, save a single dark figure that moved through the ruptured stone wall into the silent building that had stood empty for nearly forty years. Oblivious to the beauty of the night, that lone figure moved silently, intent on finding a single chamber hidden within the warren of rooms enclosed by the cold stone walls.

The figure progressed steadily through the darkness, finding its way as surely through those rooms that were utterly devoid of light as it did through those whose dirt-encrusted windows admitted just enough moonlight to illuminate their walls and doors.

The path the figure took weaved back and forth, as if it were threading its way through groupings of furniture, although each room was bare, until it came at last to a small, hidden cubicle. Others would have passed it by, for its entrance was concealed behind a panel, the sole illumination provided by the few rays of moonlight that crept through a single small window, which itself was all but invisible from beyond the Asylum's walls.

The lack of light in the chamber had no more effect on the dark-clad figure than had the blackness of the rooms through which it had already passed, for it was as familiar with the size and shape of this room as it was with the others.

Small and square, the hidden cubicle was lined with shelves, each of which contained numerous items. A museum, if you will, of the Asylum's past, containing an eclectic collection of souvenirs, the long-forgotten possessions of those who had passed through its chambers.

The figure moved from shelf to shelf, touching one artifact after another, remembering the past and the people to whom these things had once been dear.

A pair of eyes glinted in the darkness, catching the figure's attention. The memory attached to these eyes was bright and clear.

As clear as if it had happened only yesterday . . .

The child sat on her mother's lap, watching in the mirror as her mother brushed her hair, listening as her mother sang to her.

But a third face appeared in the mirror as well, for the little girl held a doll, and anyone who saw the three of them together would have noticed the resemblance.

All three—the doll, the child, and the mother—had long blond hair framing delicate, oval faces.

All three had the same lovely blue eyes.

All their cheeks glowed with rouge, and their lips shone brightly with scarlet gloss.

As the brush moved through the child's hair in long and even strokes, so also did the brush in the child's hand mimic the motions of the mother, moving through the hair of the doll with the same single-minded affection that flowed from the mother.

As her mother sang softly, the child hummed, contentedly crooning to her doll as her mother crooned to her.

Through the open window the gentle sounds of the summer afternoon lulled them. In the street, half a dozen of the neighbor boys were playing a pickup game of baseball, and in the next block the melody of the ice-cream truck chimed its tune.

The mother and child were barely aware of it, so content were they in their own little world.

Then, from downstairs, the sound of the front door slamming interrupted their idyll, and as heavy footsteps thudded on the stairs, the mother began wiping the lipstick from the child's face.

The child twisted away, dropping the brush with which she'd been stroking her doll's hair, but clutching the doll itself close to her chest. "No! I like it!" the child protested, but still the mother tried to wipe away the gloss.

Then the child's father was towering in the bedroom doorway, his face flushed with anger. When he spoke, it was with a voice so loud and harsh that both mother and child shrank away from him.

"This was not to happen again!"

The mother's eyes darted around the room as if she was seeking some avenue of escape. Finding none, she finally spoke, her voice breaking. "I'm sorry," she whispered. "I couldn't help it. I—"

"No more," her husband told her.

Again the mother's eyes darted wildly around the room. "Of course. I promise. This time—"

"This time is the last time," her husband said. Striding into the room, he swept the child from her lap, his arms closing around fragile shoulders. Though his wife reached up as if to take the child back, he moved out of her reach. "No more," he repeated. "Didn't I tell you what would happen if this continued?"

Now the woman's eyes filled with panic, and she rose to her feet. "No!" she pleaded. "Oh, God, don't! Please don't!"

"It's too late," the man told her. "You leave me no choice."

Pulling the doll from the child's arms, he tossed it onto

the bed. Then, ignoring the child's shrieks, he carried her out of the bedroom and started downstairs. Moving down the long central hall on the lower floor, he passed through the butler's pantry and the large kitchen, where the cook, frozen in silence, watched as he strode toward the back door. But before he could open it, his wife appeared, holding the doll.

"Please," she begged. "Let her take it. She loves it so. As much as I love her."

The man hesitated, and for a moment it seemed as if he would refuse. But as his child cried out in anguish and reached for the doll, he relented.

The woman watched helplessly as her husband carried her child out of the house. Instinctively, she knew she would never see her child again. And she would never be allowed to have another.

The man carried the child through the great oak doors of the Asylum, and finally set the small, trembling figure on her feet. A matron waited, and she now knelt in front of the child.

"Such a pretty little thing," she said. As the child, holding her doll, sobbed, the matron looked up at the man. "Is this all she brought with her?"

"It's more than will be necessary," the man replied. "If anything else is ever needed, please let my office know." He looked down at his child for a moment that stretched out so long a spark of hope glowed briefly in the child's eyes. Finally, he shook his head.

"I'm sorry," he said. "Sorry for what she did, and sorry you let her do it. Now there is no other way." Without touching his child again, the man turned and strode through the enormous doors.

Without being told, the child knew she would never see her father again.

When they were alone, the matron took her by the hand and led her through a long hallway and then up *some stairs. There was another long hallway, and finally she was led into a room.*

Not nearly as nice as her room at home.

This room was small, and though there was a window, it was covered with heavy metal mesh.

There was a bed, but nothing like the pretty four-poster she had at home.

There was a chair, but nothing like the rocking chair her mother had painted in her favorite shade of blue.

There was a dresser, but it was painted an ugly brown she knew her mother would have hated.

"This will be your room," the matron told her.

The child said nothing.

The matron went to the dresser and took out a plain cotton dress that looked nothing like the pretty things her mother had given her. There was also a pair of panties, and some socks that had turned an ugly gray color. "And these will be your clothes. Put them on, please."

The child hesitated, then did as the matron had instructed. Taking off the frilly pinafore in which her mother had dressed her that morning, she lay it carefully on the bed so as not to wrinkle it. Then she pulled off her underthings, and was about to put on the panties when she heard the matron utter a strange sound. Looking up, she saw the woman staring down at her naked body, her eyes wide.

"Did I do something wrong?" the child asked, speaking for the first time.

The matron hesitated, then shook her head. "No, child, of course you didn't. But we got you the wrong clothes, didn't we? Little boys don't wear dresses, do they?" The matron picked up the doll. "And they certainly don't play with dolls. We'll get rid of this right now."

The child screamed in protest, then fell sobbing to the bed, but it did no good. The matron took the doll away. The child would never see it again.

*Nor would anyone beyond the Asylum's walls ever see
the child again.*

The dark figure cradled the doll, gazing into its porcelain face in the moonlight, stroking its long blond hair,
remembering how it had come to be here. And knowing
to whom it must now be given. . . .

Chapter 1

*E*lizabeth McGuire was worried. It had now been nearly twenty-four hours since her husband had gotten the call from Jules Hartwick. Though the banker told Bill that the "small problem" that had come up about the Blackstone Center wasn't particularly serious, Bill had been brooding ever since. All through yesterday afternoon his agitation had grown worse. By dinnertime even Megan, who in the six short years of her life had rarely failed to bring a smile to her father's face, was unable to extract anything more than a grunt from him.

Bill spent most of the night pacing the house, finally coming to bed only when Elizabeth had come downstairs, rubbing her distended belly, and informed him that not only was she lonely, but their soon-to-be-born baby was too. That had at least brought Bill to bed, but she was aware that he hadn't really slept. By dawn he was already dressed and downstairs, getting in Mrs. Goodrich's way.

Worse, when Megan came down ten minutes ago, the first thing she wanted to know was if her daddy was sick. Elizabeth assured the little girl that her father was all right, but Megan wasn't convinced, and volunteered to take care of her daddy if he was sick. Only when Bill himself had given her a hug and declared that he was fine had she gone off to the kitchen to help Mrs. Goodrich with the breakfast dishes.

Now, as she poured Bill a second cup of coffee, Elizabeth tried to reassure him one more time. "If Jules Hartwick said it's nothing serious, I don't see why you don't believe him."

Bill sighed heavily. "I wish it were that simple. But everything was all set. I mean, everything, right down to the wrecking ball day before yesterday—"

"Which was mostly ceremonial," Elizabeth reminded him. "It's not like you're tearing the whole building down. You told me yourself the ball was mostly for show."

"It was still the beginning," Bill groused. "I'm telling you, Elizabeth, I just have a bad feeling about this."

"Well, you'll know in another twenty minutes," Elizabeth told him, glancing at the clock. "It'll be all right, I know it." She heaved herself up from the table, suppressing a groan. "This has to be the heaviest baby in history. It feels like it weighs forty pounds."

Bill slipped an arm around her, and together they walked to the front door. "See you in an hour or so," he said. He kissed her distractedly and was just reaching for the doorknob when the bell rang. He opened the door to the mailman, standing on the porch, holding a large package. "Another present, Charlie?" he asked. "Is this one for Christmas, or the new baby?"

The mailman smiled. "Hard to say. Christmas is only a couple of weeks away, and the package just says McGuire. Take your pick, I guess. Don't weigh too much, for whatever that's worth."

"It means I can take it," Elizabeth said, reaching for the package as Bill started down the steps. "Thank you, Charlie."

"Just doing my job."

The mailman touched his cap almost as if saluting, and Elizabeth had to resist the urge to return the salute. Contenting herself with a wave, she called a good-bye to her husband and went back into the house, quickly closing the door against the early December chill.

Taking the package back to the dining room with her,

she stared at it, puzzled. Just as Charlie had said, it bore no other name but McGuire, and their address, written in neat, block letters.

There was no return address.

" 'Curiouser and curiouser,' " she quoted softly as she tore away the brown paper that enclosed the parcel. She was just opening the box itself when Megan came in.

"What's that, Mommy? Is it for me?"

Elizabeth peered into the box, then lifted out a doll.

A beautiful, antique doll with blue glass eyes and long blond hair.

Save for the doll, the box was empty.

Her eyes went once more to the empty spot where the sender's name should have been. "How strange," Elizabeth said.

Chapter 2

*B*ill McGuire started down the hill toward the center of Blackstone. Elizabeth is right, he told himself. Whatever prompted Jules Hartwick's call yesterday morning was no more serious than Jules claimed.

"We need to have a meeting," Hartwick had explained. "And I think you should hold off on the project for a day or two, at least, until we can talk."

Though Bill had asked any number of questions, trying to find out precisely what was on the banker's mind, Hartwick refused to answer, saying only that he wasn't ready to go into it yet; that Bill shouldn't worry.

Meaningless platitudes that had triggered even louder alarms in Bill's mind. How on earth could he *not* worry? Blackstone Center was the biggest project he'd ever taken on. He'd turned down two other jobs—one in Port Arbello, the other in Eastbury—in order to concentrate on the conversion of the old Asylum into the sort of commercial center that could revive what had been a slowly dying town. The Center, in fact, had been in large part his own idea. He had thought about it for more than a year before even suggesting it to the directors of the Blackstone Trust. The one person he'd talked to almost from the start was Oliver Metcalf, because he'd known that without Oliver's support, the plan would never have gotten off the ground. A couple of tepid editorials in the *Chronicle*, and that would have been that. But Oliver was enthusiastic about the Blackstone Center from the very beginning, with a single major reservation.

"What about me?" he'd wanted to know. "Am I suddenly going to be living on the busiest street in town?"

Bill had already thought of that. Grabbing a pencil from Oliver's cluttered desk, he'd quickly sketched a rough map to show that the most logical approach to the site was not through the front gates, but from the back, where the old service entrance had once been. Appeased, Oliver immediately backed the project, pushing for it not only in the paper, but with his uncle as well. Once Harvey Connally had been won over—albeit reluctantly—the rest was easy. By the day before yesterday, when the wrecker's ball had made its ceremonial swing, puncturing the Asylum's west wall in preparation for the expansion of the building, most of the opposition to the project had evaporated.

Bill McGuire, and his entire crew, had been all set to go to work the next day.

Yesterday.

But only hours after the ceremony, Jules Hartwick made his ominous call. "Hold off for a day or two," indeed! "Not to worry"—fat chance of that. Bill McGuire was worried, all right. Worried nearly out of his mind.

Now, as he walked the three blocks down Amherst Street to the corner of Main, where the redbrick, Federal-style building that housed the First National Bank of Blackstone stood, he felt an anticipatory rush of fear. His nerves gave an additional jump when he spotted Oliver Metcalf at the bank's door.

"You know what this is all about?" Oliver asked.

"He called you too?" Bill replied, trying to betray nothing of his ballooning sense that something very serious had gone wrong.

"Yesterday. But he wouldn't say what it was about, which tells me that whatever it is, it's not good news."

"Did he tell you not to worry?"

The editor nodded. His eyes searched McGuire's face. "You don't have any idea at all what this is about?"

McGuire glanced in both directions, but they seemed to be alone on the sidewalk. "All he told me was to hold off on the Center project. You can guess how that made me feel."

"Yes," Oliver said with an ironic smile, "I certainly can."

Together the two men entered the bank, nodded to the tellers who stood behind old-fashioned frosted-glass windows, and made their way to Jules Hartwick's office at the back.

"Mr. Hartwick and Mr. Becker are waiting for you," Ellen Golding told them. "You can go on in."

Bill and Oliver exchanged another glance. What was Hartwick planning to tell them that required the presence of his lawyer?

Jules Hartwick was on his feet as they entered the walnut-paneled office, and he came around from behind his desk to greet both men with no less warmth than ever. The gesture did nothing to ease Bill McGuire's sense of foreboding. He'd learned long ago that a warm handshake and a friendly smile meant absolutely nothing in the world of banking. Sure enough, as Hartwick retreated around his desk and lowered himself into his deeply tufted red-leather swivel chair, his smile faded. "I don't suppose there's any easy way to tell you this," he began, looking from Bill McGuire to Oliver Metcalf, then back again.

"I assume it has to do with the financing for the Blackstone Center project, right?" the contractor asked, his worst fears congealing into a hard knot in his belly.

The banker took a deep breath, then slowly let it out. "I wish it were that simple," he said. "If it were only the Center project, I suspect I could arrange a bridge loan for a few—"

"Bridge loan?" McGuire interrupted. "For Christ's sake, Jules, why would I need a bridge loan?" He rose from his chair, his hands unconsciously clenching into fists. "The financing's supposed to be all set!" But even as he spoke the words, McGuire knew that no matter how true they might have been only a few days ago, they no longer were. Nor would getting angry help the situation. "Sorry," he said, slumping back into his chair. "So what is it? What's happened?"

"We don't really think it's very serious," Ed Becker said, but there was something in his tone that told both McGuire and Oliver Metcalf that whatever was coming was going to be very bad indeed. "The Federal Reserve has put a temporary hold on loans by the bank, and—"

"Excuse me?" Oliver Metcalf cut in. "Did you say the Federal Reserve?" His eyes shifted from the lawyer to the banker. "What exactly is going on, Jules?"

Jules Hartwick shifted uncomfortably in his chair. For twenty years, ever since he'd taken over the bank after his father suddenly died, the worst part of the job had been having to tell a customer—usually someone he'd known most of his life—that he couldn't give him a loan. But this was worse.

Far worse.

The construction account had already been set up; the first funds had been transferred into it. And Bill McGuire had already begun hiring a crew; two of the men who would be working on the project, Tom Cleary and Jim Nicholson, had come into the bank only yesterday to make small payments on debts the bank had been carrying for months. Just as he—and his father before him—always had, Jules told both men to wait until after Christmas. What, after all, could be the harm? The bank had already been carrying Tommy for a year and a half, and Jim for nine months.

What would another month matter?

Let the men and their families enjoy the holiday.

Except that now there would be no more paychecks for those men, for the simple reason that the routine audit the

Federal Reserve was working on had turned up what it considered a "disproportionately large percentage" of inactive loans.

So many, in fact, that the Fed had put a hold on all new lending by the Blackstone bank until the bank could demonstrate how it was going to handle the loans.

But to Jules Hartwick, they weren't simply "inactive loans." They were loans to people he'd known all his life, people who had worked hard and always done their best to meet their responsibilities. Not one of them had purposely quit a job, or been lax in looking for a new one. They had simply been caught in an economy that was "downsizing"—a word Jules Hartwick had come to hate—and would make good on their debts the moment things got better for them.

Now, thanks to his own decision to carry all those loans, the bank wasn't going to be able to fund the Center project. Ironically, the Fed had seen to it that at least some of the men whose loans were a source of concern to the auditors would no longer have the jobs that would allow them to make their loans current.

"It seems the auditors are worried about the way we do business," he said, forcing himself to meet Bill McGuire's gaze straight on. "For the moment, we're going to be unable to continue funding the construction account." He turned to Oliver Metcalf. "The reason I wanted you here is so that Ed can explain exactly what's happening. The bank isn't insolvent, and I'm sure we'll be able to straighten all this out in a couple of weeks. But if word gets out that the Fed is nervous about us—well, I'm sure you can imagine what would happen."

"A run," Oliver said. "Could you stand one?"

Jules Hartwick shrugged. "Probably. If it got bad, we might lose our independence. In the end, none of our depositors would lose a cent, but we'd be folded into one of the big regional banks and become just one more small branch with no flexibility to do things our way."

"Your way seems to have gotten us all into a fine mess, if you ask me," Bill McGuire said. "What am I supposed to tell my people, Jules? That the jobs they've been counting on have simply evaporated? Not to mention my own job." Though this time he managed to stay in his chair, his voice began to rise. "Do you have any idea how much work I turned down to make this project happen? Any idea at all? I'm already stretched tight, Jules. The new baby's due in a month, and I—" Abruptly, he cut short the tirade he'd been working up to, recognizing the genuine pain the banker was feeling. What, after all, was the point of yelling at Jules? Once again he forced himself to calm down. "Do you have any idea how long it might be?" he asked in a more reasonable voice. "Is this just a temporary funding freeze, or is the project done for?"

Hartwick was silent for a long time, but finally spread his hands helplessly. "I don't know," he said. "I'm hoping it's only for a week or so, but I can't promise you anything." He hesitated, then forced himself to finish. "There's a possibility it could be months."

The banker kept talking in an effort to explain, but Bill McGuire was no longer listening. Instead his mind was already working, trying to figure out what to do next.

This afternoon he'd drive up to Port Arbello and see if there was any chance of bidding on the condominium project he'd turned down three weeks ago. Although that project wasn't supposed to start until spring, if he could secure the job, its financing would tide them over for a while. And while he was up there, maybe he'd talk to the developers behind the condo project about finding new financing for the Blackstone Project.

"Well, what do you think?" he asked Oliver Metcalf twenty minutes later as they left the bank. "Is it all over even before it starts?"

Metcalf shook his head. "Not if I have anything to do with it. All I'm going to run is a small article to the effect that the project is being held up, maybe imply that there are some permits not in place yet. Then we'll see what happens."

Nodding, McGuire turned away and started up Amherst Street. He hadn't taken more than a couple of steps when Metcalf called out to him.

"Bill? Give my love to Elizabeth and Megan. And try not to worry. Things will work out."

McGuire forced a smile, wishing he could share Oliver Metcalf's optimism.

Chapter 3

*O*liver Metcalf was already starting to compose his editorial as he left the bank building, but instead of going directly back to his office, he turned in the opposite direction, walking a block farther down Main Street to the corner of Princeton, where the old Carnegie Library still stood in the center of the half acre of land that Harvey Connally's father had donated nearly a century ago. Though most of the old Carnegie libraries that had sprung up in small towns all over the country had been replaced decades ago by far more modern "media centers," the one in Blackstone remained as unchanged as the rest of the town. Part of the reason for its preservation was Blackstone's sense of historic pride; part was lack of funds for modernization. Though there were a few new buildings—"new" being defined as less than fifty years old—most of the town still looked as it had a hundred years ago, some peeling paint and other signs of wear and tear notwithstanding; and some of it had gone unchanged for more than two centuries.

In Oliver Metcalf's own memory, nothing about the library had changed at all. Perhaps the trees were a little bigger than they'd been when he was a boy, but even then the maples on the front lawn had been fairly mature, spreading their limbs wide, providing plenty of shade for the Story Lady, who had read to the children of the town every Thursday afternoon of the summer months. Now, forty years later, there was still a Story Lady, and she still entranced the children of Blackstone on warm summer Thursdays. Oliver suspected there would always be a Story Lady. Anyway, he hoped so.

Today, though, there was no storyteller or cluster of children in evidence as Oliver mounted the steep flight of concrete steps, deeply worn by generations of feet moving up and down, and pushed through the outer set of double doors that provided a buffer between the chill of the December day outside and the comforting heat from the old-fashioned radiators whose occasional clanging was the loudest sound ever heard within the walls of the building. The radiators provided too much heat, really, but nobody objected because Germaine Wagner, who had been the head librarian for nearly twenty years now, always insisted, "A warm room leads to the appreciation of good books." Oliver had never been able to figure out what the connection between temperature and literature might be, but Germaine was willing to work for a salary that was no more modern than the building itself; if she wanted the heat turned up, so be it.

Now, as Oliver pushed through the second set of doors, Germaine looked up from the stack of books she was checking back into the library—still with old-fashioned cards bearing the due date and the signatures of the people who had borrowed them tucked into envelopes glued to the inside covers. Peering at Oliver over the tops of her half-glasses, Germaine stuck her pencil into the thick bun of hair that was neatly pinned to the top of her head and beckoned him over to the desk.

"I'm hearing rumors that there might be a problem with Blackstone Center," she said in the professional whisper with which she could silence rowdy high school students from seventy feet away.

Oliver's mind went over the possibilities. He supposed that Germaine had seen him go into the bank with Bill McGuire and immediately assumed the worst. The assumption would have been typical of her. Or someone else had seen them and told Germaine.

More likely, Germaine was on a fishing expedition, looking for a juicy tidbit to take home to her mother. Old Clara Wagner, wheelchair bound, hadn't been out of the house in at least a decade, but she loved a good piece of gossip even more than Germaine.

To say nothing at all to Germaine was tantamount to guaranteeing that whatever rumor she passed on would henceforth have his name attached to it ("I asked Oliver Metcalf point-blank, and he did *not* deny it!"), so he decided the best thing to do would be to send her off in the wrong direction. "Well, I know Bill's been pretty busy with some other projects," Oliver said. "I suspect that once he gets them wound up, he'll be pitching into the Asylum full-tilt."

Germaine pursed her lips suspiciously. "It seems to me that leaving equipment idle up there is something Bill McGuire wouldn't do," she replied, her sharp eyes boring into him. "He's never been one to waste a dime, Oliver."

"Well, I'm sure he knows what he's doing," Oliver said. Then, before the librarian's cross-examination could continue, he rushed on. "Actually, the Center project is the reason I came by. I'm thinking of running a series on the history of the building."

The librarian fixed on him darkly. "I would have thought you'd have all the material you need right in your own house," she observed, "given who your father was."

Suddenly, Oliver felt like a little boy who'd come to school without his homework. "I'm afraid my father didn't keep much in the way of memorabilia," he said.

The librarian's eyes narrowed slightly, and her already narrow nostrils took on a pinched look. "No, I don't suppose he would have, would he?" There was a coldness in her tone that made Oliver flinch, but he tried to pretend that neither the look nor the words affected him.

Just as he'd tried all his life to pretend that looks and words such as Germaine Wagner's had no effect on him.

"It's only gossip, Oliver," his uncle had told him over and over again. "They have no more idea of what really happened than anyone else. The best thing to do is simply ignore them. Sooner or later they'll find other things to talk about." His uncle had been right. As the years had gone by, fewer and fewer people gave him that curious look, or tried to ask him thinly veiled questions about what had *really* happened to his sister all those years ago. But of course Oliver had never known any more about it than anyone else. By the time he'd come home from college and gone to work for the paper, it had all but been forgotten.

Except that every now and then, with people like Germaine Wagner, he still found that a look could slice open old wounds, a tone of voice could sting. But there was nothing he could do about it; like Oliver himself, the Germaines of this world were going to have to go to their graves still not knowing the truth.

"I really don't remember that much about my father," he said carefully now. "Which, I suppose, is part of why I'm here. I thought that maybe now that the Asylum's finally going to be put to a good use, it might be time for me to write up a history of how it came to be here in the first place."

"Caring for the mentally ill was a perfectly good use for the building," Germaine replied. "My mother was very proud of her work there."

"As she should have been," Oliver quickly assured her. "But it's been so long since it was closed that I really don't know much about it myself. And I suspect that whatever historical material still exists is upstairs in the attic here. I thought I'd see what I could find."

He waited as the librarian pondered his request. Germaine Wagner, over the years, had come to think of the contents of the library as her personal property, and tended to consider so much as a one-day-overdue book as a personal affront. As to letting someone paw through the boxes and boxes of old documents, diaries, and memoirs that had migrated into the library over the course of the eight decades since it had been built, Oliver suspected that she would take his request as an invasion of her privacy.

"Well, I don't suppose there's any real reason why you shouldn't be able to see what's there," Germaine finally said in a sorrowful tone as if she was already regretting having to make the admission. "I suppose I could have Rebecca bring down whatever we have."

As if the librarian's mere mention of her name was enough to summon her, a girl appeared from the back room.

Except that she wasn't a girl; not really. Rebecca Morrison was in her late twenties, with a heart-shaped face that radiated a sweet innocence, framed by soft chestnut hair that fell in waves from a part in the center. Her eyes, slightly tilted, were a deep brown, and utterly guileless.

Oliver had known her since she was a child, and when he'd had to write the obituary after the automobile accident that left sixteen-year-old Rebecca an orphan, tears had streamed down his face. For weeks after the fatal car crash, Rebecca hovered between life and death. Though there were many people in Blackstone who had fallen into the habit of referring to her as "Poor Rebecca," Oliver was not among them. It had taken months for the girl to recover from her injuries, and while it was true that when she emerged from the hospital her smile was sad and her mind was slower, to Oliver the sweetness that imbued Rebecca's personality more than made up for the slight intellectual damage she had suffered in the accident.

Now, as she smiled at him, he felt the familiar sense of comfort her presence always gave him.

"Oliver wants to see if there is any information about the Blackstone Asylum in the attic," Germaine Wagner briskly explained. "I told him I wasn't certain, but that perhaps you could look."

"Oh, there's a whole box of things," Rebecca said, and Oliver was sure he saw a flash of disapproval in the librarian's eyes. "I'll bring it down right away."

"I'll help you," Oliver immediately volunteered.

"You don't have to," Rebecca protested. "I can do it."

"But I want to," Oliver insisted.

As he followed Rebecca to the stairs leading up to the mezzanine and the attic beyond, he felt the librarian's eyes following him, and had to resist the urge to turn around and glare at her. After all, he thought, most of her problem undoubtedly stemmed from the simple fact that in her whole life, no man had probably ever followed her up the stairs.

Ten minutes later a large dusty box filled with file folders, photo albums, letters, and diaries was sitting on one of the immense oak tables that were lined up in two precise rows in the front of the library, close by the windows. Oliver settled onto one of the hard oak chairs, reached into the box, and pulled out a photo album. Setting it on the table in front of him, he opened it at random.

And found himself staring at a picture of his father.

The photograph had been taken years ago, long before Oliver had been born. In it, Malcolm Metcalf stood in front of the doors of the Asylum, his arms folded across his chest, scowling straight into the camera almost as if he were challenging it.

Challenging it to what? Oliver wondered.

And yet, as he stared at the black-and-white photograph, he felt a shudder take form inside him. As though it were Oliver himself who had brought forth Malcolm Metcalf's piercing look of disapproval.

But, of course, it was the unseen photographer upon whom his father had fixed that look; he had not wanted the camera any closer to the Asylum than it already was.

In the photograph, Malcolm Metcalf was guarding the doors of his Asylum against the prying eye of the camera.

Oliver flipped the pages quickly, as if to escape his father's stern stare, when suddenly an image seemed to leap forth from the pages of the book.

A boy is tied down to a bed.
His hands are tied, his ankles are strapped.
Across his torso, a shadow falls.
The boy is screaming. . . .

Blinking, and shaking his head, Oliver quickly flipped back through the pages, searching for the picture.

Only there was no such picture in the book.

Chapter 4

As he had often done before, Bill McGuire paused on the sidewalk in front of his house for no better reason than to gaze in satisfaction upon the structure in which he'd spent almost all his life. The house was a Victorian—the only one on this particular block of Amherst Street—and though Bill was perfectly well aware of the current fashion of turning houses such as his into pink, purple, or lavender Painted Ladies, neither he nor Elizabeth had ever been tempted to coat the old house with half a dozen colors of paint. Instead, they had faithfully maintained the earthy tones—mustards, tans, greens, and maroons—of the period, and the elaborate white trim, meant by the original builders to resemble lace that gave the house a feeling of lightness, despite its mass.

The house was one of only six on the block, and all of them had been as well taken care of as the McGuires'. Amherst Street, which sloped gently up the hill, eventually turning to the left, then back to the right, and finally ending at the gates of the old Asylum, could easily have been set aside as a sort of living museum of architecture. There was a large half-timbered Tudor on one side of the McGuires', and a good example of Federal on the other. On the opposite side of the street were two houses that had been built early in the Craftsman era, separated by a large saltbox that, to Bill at least, appeared slightly embarrassed by the Victorian effusiveness of its across-the-street neighbor. Still, all six houses sat on spacious enough grounds and were surrounded by so many trees and shrubs that the block was unified by its parklike look, if not its architecture.

Today, though, as he gazed up at his house, with its profusion of steeply pitched roofs and dormer windows, Bill had a strange sense that something was not right. He searched the structure for some clue to his uneasiness, but could see nothing wrong. The paint wasn't peeling, nor were any shingles missing. He quickly scanned the ornate trim work that he'd always taken special pride in keeping in perfect repair, but every bit of it looked exactly as it should. Not a spindle missing, nor a lath either split or broken. Telling himself his discomfort was nothing more than his own bad mood after the meeting at the bank, Bill strode up the brick pathway, mounted the steps that led to the high front porch, and went inside.

The sense that something was wrong grew stronger.

"Elizabeth?" he called out. "Megan? Anybody home?" For a moment he heard nothing at all, then the door leading to the butler's pantry at the far end of the dining room opened and he saw Mrs. Goodrich's stooped form shuffling toward him.

"They're both upstairs," the old woman said. "You might want to go up and talk to the missus. I think she might be a little upset. And I'm fixing some lunch for the whole family." The old woman, who had been with Elizabeth since she was a child in Port Arbello, gazed at him worriedly. "You'll be here, won't you?"

"I'll be here, Mrs. Goodrich," he assured her. As the housekeeper made her slow way back to the kitchen, Bill started up the stairs. Before he was even halfway to the second-floor landing, Megan appeared, gazing down at him with dark, uncertain eyes.

"Why can't I have my dolly?" she demanded. "Why won't Mommy give her to me?"

"Dolly?" Bill repeated. "What dolly are you talking about?"

"The one someone sent me," Megan said. Her eyes narrowed slightly. "Mommy won't let me have her."

At that moment Elizabeth, still dressed in the night-gown and robe she'd been wearing when Bill left the house three hours earlier, appeared behind their daughter, smiling wanly. "Honey, it's not that I won't let you have the doll. It's just that we don't know who it's for."

"Would one of you mind enlightening me about what's going on?" Bill asked as he came to the top of the stairs. He knelt down to give Megan a kiss, then stood and slid his arm around his wife. The smile his kiss had put on Megan's face disappeared.

"It's for me!" she declared. "When you see it, you'll know."

"Come on," Elizabeth said. "It's in our room. I'll show it to you."

With Megan reaching up to put her hand in his, Bill followed his wife into the big master bedroom. On the old chaise longue, once his mother's favorite place to sit and read, was the box the mailman had delivered this morning. Reaching into it, Elizabeth lifted out the doll, automatically cradling it in her arms as if it were a baby. "It's really very beautiful," she said as Bill moved closer to her. "I think its face must be hand-painted, and the clothes look like they were handmade too."

Bill looked down into the doll's face, which had been painted so perfectly that for the briefest of moments he almost had the feeling the doll was looking back up at him. "Who on earth sent it?"

Elizabeth shrugged. "That's the problem. Not only wasn't there any return address, but there wasn't any card with it either."

"It's mine!" Megan piped, reaching up for the doll. "Why would anybody send a doll to a grown-up?"

Elizabeth, seeming to hold the doll a little closer to her breast, turned away from the little girl. "But we don't know that it was sent to you, darling. It might be a present for the new baby."

Megan scowled deeply and her chin began to tremble. "But the baby's going to be a boy," she said. "You said so. And boys don't play with dollies!"

"We *hope* the baby is going to be a boy," Elizabeth explained. "But we don't know. And if you have a little sister, don't you think she'll love the doll as much as you do?"

Megan's features took on a look of intransigence that almost made Bill laugh. "No," she declared. "Babies don't even play with dolls. All they do is eat and cry and wet their diapers." She turned to her father, and her eyes opened wide. "Please, Daddy, can't I have her?"

"I'll tell you what," Bill said. "Why don't we put the doll away for a while and see if we can find out who sent it? Then, if it turns out it was meant for you, it'll be yours. And if it turns out it was meant for the baby, we'll wait until the baby is born, and if it's a little boy, then the doll can be your first present from your little brother. How does that sound?"

Megan looked uncertain. "Where are we going to put her?"

Bill thought for a moment. "What about the hall closet, downstairs?"

Megan brightened. "All right," she agreed. "But I get to carry her downstairs."

"Sounds fair enough," Bill agreed. He winked at Elizabeth. "After all, you've gotten to have it all morning. Don't you think it's only fair that Megan should get to carry it?"

For a moment he almost thought he saw hesitation in his wife's eyes, as if she wasn't quite ready to give up the doll, but then she smiled. "Of course," she agreed. She knelt down and handed the doll to Megan. "But you have to cradle it, just like I did. Even though it's not a real baby, you could hurt it if you dropped it, and it's very valuable."

"I won't drop her," Megan declared, holding the antique doll close to her chest just the way her mother had a moment earlier. "I love her."

Together, the family went downstairs and opened the hall closet. "She'll get cold in here," Megan said. "We have to wrap her in a blanket." She darted back up the stairs, returning a minute later with the small pink blanket that had first been in her crib, and since then at the foot of her bed. "She can use this," she said, carefully wrapping the doll in the blanket. Then she surrendered it to her father, who put it up on the shelf, nested among the woolen ski caps, gloves, and scarves.

"There," he said. "Now she'll sleep until we find out who she belongs to." But as they moved toward the dining room, where Mrs. Goodrich was putting their lunch on the table, he saw Megan turn back to look longingly at the closet.

He had a suspicion that before the afternoon was over, the doll would somehow have found its way from the closet to his daughter's room.

That, however, would be something Elizabeth would have to deal with, since he himself would be in Port Arbello.

"Do you really have to go?" Elizabeth asked when he told her what had happened at the bank that morning and what he had to do now.

"If we want to eat, I do. I'm pretty sure I can still get the job. But I'm probably going to have to hole up in a motel for the night, putting together numbers so I can nail it down in the morning." He glanced at his wife's swollen belly, which seemed—impossibly—to have grown even larger just in the few hours he'd been gone. "Will you be all right?"

"I have a whole month yet before he's due," Elizabeth said, instantly reading his thoughts. "Believe me, I'm not going to deliver early just because you're out of town. So go, do what you have to do, and don't worry about Megan and me. Mrs. Goodrich has been taking care of me all my life. She can do it one more night."

"Mrs. Goodrich is almost ninety," Bill reminded her. "She shouldn't even be working."

"Try telling her that," Elizabeth replied, laughing. "She'll eat you for supper!"

An hour later, when he was ready to take his overnight bag and portable computer out to the car, Bill's earlier uneasiness returned. "Maybe I better not go," he said. "Maybe I can do it all over the phone."

"You know you can't," Elizabeth said firmly. "Go on! Nothing's going to happen to us."

But even as he drove away from the house, Bill found himself looking back at it.

Looking back, and still feeling that something was wrong.

Chapter 5

*E*lizabeth was holding her baby—a perfect, tiny boy—cradling him gently against her breast. She was sitting on the porch, in a rocking chair, but it wasn't the porch of the house in Blackstone, nor, oddly, was the day nearly as cold as it should have been, with Christmas only three weeks away.

The summer mists seemed to part, and she realized where she was—back home in Port Arbello, on the porch of the old house on Conger's Point, and it was a perfect July day. A cool wind was blowing in off the sea, and the sound of surf breaking against the base of the bluff was lulling her baby into a contented sleep. She began humming softly, just loud enough so her baby could hear her, but quietly enough not to disturb him.

> "Rockabye baby,
> In the tree tops,
> When the wind blows,
> The cradle will rock . . ."

The words died away to nothing more than a murmuring hum, and Elizabeth began to feel drowsy, her eyelids heavy. But then, just as the song faded completely from her lips, a movement caught her eye.

A child was emerging from the woods across the field. Megan.

Elizabeth was about to call out to her daughter, but as

the child grew closer, she realized this little girl wasn't blond, sunny Megan at all.

It was her sister.

It was Sarah!

But that wasn't possible, for Sarah looked no older now than she had on that day so many years ago when she'd been taken away to the hospital.

Yet as the little girl drew closer, walking steadily across the field, directly toward her, Elizabeth felt a terrible chill.

Sarah was carrying something cradled in her arms. She was holding it out now, offering it to her, and Elizabeth recognized it instantly.

An arm.

Jimmy Tyler's arm . . .

Reflexively, Elizabeth looked down at her baby.

Her son was no longer sleeping. Instead, his eyes were wide open, and he was screaming, though no sound came out of his mouth. But worse than the silent scream, worse than the terror in the infant's eyes, was the blood spurting from her child's left shoulder, where the arm had been hacked away.

Elizabeth felt a scream rise from her lungs, but at the same time a terrible constriction closed her throat, and her howl of anguish stayed trapped within her, filling her up, making her feel as if she might explode into a million fragmented pieces. There was blood everywhere now, and Sarah, still holding the bloody arm that had been torn from the baby's body, was drawing closer and closer.

Elizabeth tried to turn away; could not. Finally, with an effort that seemed to sap every ounce of her energy, she hurled herself out of the chair and—

Elizabeth jerked awake. For an instant the terrible vision still hung before her. Her heart was pounding and she was gasping for breath. But as the dream quickly retreated, and as the hammering of her heart eased and her breathing returned to normal, she realized she wasn't back in Port Arbello at all.

She was in her room in Blackstone, on a December afternoon, and her baby was still safe in her womb. Yet, as if from a great distance, she once again heard the lullaby she had been crooning in the dream.

> "When the bough breaks,
> The cradle will fall,
> And down will go baby,
> Cradle and all . . ."

Elizabeth rose from the chaise on which she'd been sleeping and stepped out into the hall. The lullaby was louder now, and coming from Megan's room. Moving silently down the wide corridor that ran two-thirds of the length of the second floor, Elizabeth paused outside her daughter's door and listened.

She could still hear Megan, humming softly.

As she herself had been humming.

She opened the door a crack and peered inside.

Megan was sitting on her bed.

She was cradling the antique doll in her arms.

Elizabeth pushed the door wide. The lullaby died on Megan's lips as her eyes widened in surprise. Her arms tightened reflexively, pressing the doll close to her chest.

Elizabeth crossed the room until she was standing over her daughter. "We decided the doll would stay in the closet, didn't we?"

Megan shook her head. "You decided," she said. "I didn't."

"We all decided," Elizabeth told her. "Daddy, and Mommy, and you. So I'm going to put the doll away again. Do you understand?"

"But I want her," Megan protested. "I love her."

Reaching down, Elizabeth took the doll from her daughter. "She's not yours to love, Megan. Not yet. Perhaps someday, perhaps even someday soon. But not now. I'm putting it back in the closet," she said. "And you're not to touch it again. Do you understand?"

Megan looked up, saying nothing as Elizabeth left the room and closed the door. For a moment Megan felt hot tears flood her eyes. Then she realized: It didn't matter where her mother hid the doll. She would find it, and it would be hers.

Elizabeth carried the doll back downstairs and was about to put it back in the closet when she changed her mind. The closet would be the first place Megan would look. Leaving the hall, she went through the arched entry into the living room, then beyond it, in the library, saw the perfect place to put the doll: the top shelf of one of the pair of mahogany cases Bill had built to stand on either side of the fireplace.

The top shelf—one she could barely reach herself— was empty. Even if Megan spotted the doll up there, she wouldn't be able to get to it without a ladder. Positioning the doll as far back on the shelf as she could, Elizabeth was about to leave the library and return upstairs when her eyes fell on a portrait.

Along with the treasured books Elizabeth had brought with her from Port Arbello, there were framed pictures of her family and Bill's, and even an old Ouija board she and Sarah had played with when they were children. The portrait to which her eyes had been drawn was of one of Bill's aunts—the one named Laurette, Elizabeth dimly remembered, who had killed herself long before Bill had been born. Though Elizabeth had seen the portrait dozens of times before, this time something about it caught her eye. She stared at it, trying to understand what had captured her attention. Then her eyes returned to the doll that now sat on the top shelf of the mahogany case.

There was an odd resemblance between the doll and the woman in the portrait, Elizabeth realized.

The same blue eyes.

The same long blond hair.

The same pink cheeks and red lips.

It was as if the doll were a miniature version of the woman in the painting.

A thought flitted through Elizabeth's mind. Could it be possible that the doll had actually been modeled on this woman? Perhaps even been owned by her? As quickly as the thought came, Elizabeth dismissed it.

Going back upstairs, she stretched out on the chaise once more, and this time, when she slept, she didn't dream.

Megan McGuire's eyes opened in the darkness. For a moment she was startled, unsure what had awakened her, but then, on the far wall of her bedroom, she saw a shape.

The shape of a witch, inky black, with pointed hat and flowing gown, astride a long broomstick. In her hand—held high aloft—she grasped a sword.

The witch was moving now, flying higher, moving up toward the ceiling, hurtling through the air, then down toward Megan.

The little girl shrank into her pillow, pulling the covers tight around her neck as a shiver of fear passed through her.

Closer and closer the witch came, sword brandished.

Megan pressed deeper into the pillow.

Then, just as Megan could feel the first tingling of the sorceress's touch, the apparition vanished as suddenly as it had come, snatched away by an enormous flash of light.

As she always did, Megan lay still for a moment, savoring the delicious thrill that the shadow always gave her, even though she knew perfectly well that the soaring witch was no more than a momentary vision produced by a car driving up Amherst Street, then vanquished by its headlights the instant the car passed by the house.

The room returned to its familiar shape as the sound of

the car faded away, but as Megan released her grip on the blanket that covered her, she heard something else.

A sound so soft she almost couldn't hear it at all.

The sound grew louder as she listened, and then she knew exactly what it was.

Someone was crying.

A little girl with long blond hair, pink cheeks, and blue eyes.

A little girl wearing a ruffled white pinafore and a garland of flowers in her hair.

A little girl who wanted to be her friend, but whom her mommy had sent away.

Getting up from her bed, Megan pulled her robe over her flannel nightgown and slipped her feet into the woolly slippers Mrs. Goodrich had given her for Christmas last year. Pulling the door to her room open a crack, she peered out into the hallway. Farther down the hall, halfway to the stairs, she could see the door to her parents' room.

It was closed, and no light shone from the crack beneath it.

Silently, Megan crept along the hall, then down the stairs.

The little girl's crying was louder now. When Megan reached the bottom of the stairs, she peered through the dining room and butler's pantry, into the kitchen.

No light came from any of the rooms, nor could she hear the television droning in Mrs. Goodrich's room.

Save for the sound of the little girl's sobbing, the house was as silent as it was dark.

A last, sorrowful sob faded away, and a moment later Megan heard something else.

A voice calling her name.

"Megan . . . Megan . . . Megan . . ."

It was as if the voice had become a beacon. Megan followed it away from the kitchen and the housekeeper's quarters to the other side of the house. Through the darkness of the entry hall, she moved, through the deep shadows of the large living room, gliding as easily as if it were daylight, then pausing at the door to the library.

The voice grew louder: *"Megan . . . Megan . . ."*

The library was almost pitch-black. Megan stood in the darkness, listening. Then, through the French doors leading to the flagstoned side patio, the first rays of the rising moon crept into the room. In that first instant of faint illumination, Megan saw them.

The eyes of the doll, gleaming in the moonlight, gazing down at her from the top shelf of the tall case that stood against the wall to the right of the fireplace.

So high that her mother thought she wouldn't be able to reach it.

But Megan knew better. As silent and surefooted as she'd been when she crept through the upstairs hall and down the stairs, she crossed the library and began climbing up the shelves of the cabinet as easily as if they were the steps of a ladder.

Elizabeth jerked awake, not from the terror of another nightmare, but from a loud crash, immediately followed by a terrified shriek. Then, a long, wailing cry.

Megan!

Heaving herself out of bed and ignoring the robe lying on the chaise longue, Elizabeth stumbled through the darkness toward the bedroom door. She fumbled with the two old-fashioned light switches set in the wall next to the door. A second later the overhead fixture in the center of the ceiling came on, filling the room with harsh white light. Blinking in the glare, Elizabeth jerked the bedroom door open and stepped into the hall, now lit brightly with its own three chandeliers.

Megan's door was closed, but as Elizabeth started toward her daughter's room, another scream rent the night.

Downstairs!

Megan had gone downstairs and—

The doll! She'd found the doll and tried to get it, and—

Heart beating wildly, Elizabeth lurched to the top of the long flight and started down. When she was still three steps from the bottom, the lights in the entry hall came on, illuminating Mrs. Goodrich, wrapped in a tattered chenille bathrobe, shuffling toward the living room.

As still another cry echoed through the house, Elizabeth came to the bottom of the stairs and rushed through the living room. At the door to the library, she reached for the bank of switches, pressing every one her fingers touched. As the lights flashed on and every shadow was washed from the room, the vision Elizabeth had seen only in her mind a few moments before was now revealed in its terrible reality.

The mahogany case had fallen forward. Beneath it, Elizabeth could see Megan struggling to free herself from the massive weight pressing down on her. The pictures and curios that had filled the case's shelves were scattered everywhere, shards of glass from broken picture frames littered the carpet, and figurines lay broken all around her.

Megan's shrieks had deepened to a sobbing cry.

Choking back a scream, Elizabeth rushed across the room and bent down, her fingers curling around the front edge of the cabinet's top.

From the doorway, realizing what Elizabeth was about to do, Mrs. Goodrich cried out. "Don't! You mustn't!"

Ignoring the old housekeeper's plea, Elizabeth summoned every ounce of strength she could muster and heaved the case upward, lifting it off her daughter. "Move, Megan," Elizabeth cried. "Get out from—" Her words cut off by a terrible flash of pain that felt as if a knife had been thrust into her belly, Elizabeth struggled to hold on to the cabinet while Megan, finally responding to her mother's voice, squirmed free. A second later the weight of the cabinet overwhelmed her and it crashed back to the floor. Elizabeth sank down onto the carpet as another wrenching pain ripped through her and she felt something inside her give way.

"Call . . . ambulance," she gasped, her hands clutching protectively at her belly. "Oh, God, Mrs. Goodrich. Hurry!"

Wave after wave of pain was crushing her. Elizabeth felt a terrible weakness come over her, and the light began to fade.

The last thing she saw before darkness closed around her was Megan, on her feet now and looking down at her.

In Megan's arms, utterly undamaged by the accident that had smashed everything else the cabinet had held, was the doll.

Chapter 6

*B*ill McGuire turned into the nearly deserted parking lot of Blackstone Memorial Hospital and pulled the car into the space closest to the emergency entrance. He'd driven for nearly three hours, leaving the motel in Port Arbello minutes after he'd gotten the call from Mrs. Goodrich, pausing only long enough to drop the room key through the mail slot in the office's locked front door. Throughout the frantic drive to Blackstone, he'd had to force himself time and again to slow down, reminding himself that the objective was to get home as quickly as possible, but in one piece. Still, the drive seemed endless. He managed to reach the hospital three times on his cellular phone, but all three connections ended in a frustrating crackle of static.

All he'd been able to find out was that Elizabeth had gone into labor, and that things were "going as well as can be expected."

Oh dear God, let her live, he prayed. Dear merciful God, let the baby be all right.

Oh God, why, *why* did I have to leave them tonight, of all nights?

Tensed over the wheel, he felt sharp, stabbing needles of guilt as he raced through the darkness, returning from a trip that now seemed utterly unnecessary. He'd won the condo project, but even while putting together the final figures in the motel room, he'd known he could have done the whole thing on the phone from his desk in the library at home.

Slamming the car door behind him, barely able to wait for the automatic glass doors to open for him, Bill raced into the waiting room and immediately spotted Mrs. Goodrich, still wearing her old chenille bathrobe, sitting on a sagging green-plastic upholstered sofa, her arm wrapped protectively around Megan, whose forehead was partially covered by a bandage. Mrs. Goodrich, in her fear for the welfare of the person she loved best in the world, looked almost as small as Megan, but as Bill approached he saw a determined glimmer in the old woman's eyes, and she made a gesture as if to shoo him away.

"We're all right," she told him. "Just a little cut on Megan's forehead, but it doesn't even hurt anymore, does it, darlin'?"

Megan bobbed her head. "I just fell off the shelves, that's all," she said in a small voice.

"You go see to Elizabeth," Mrs. Goodrich went on. "We'll be right here. You tell Elizabeth we're praying for her."

A few seconds later Bill was following a doctor down the hall, listening to a brief explanation of what had happened. Then he was in the room where Elizabeth lay in bed, her face ashen, her blond hair, darkened only slightly over the years, spread around her head like a halo.

As if sensing that at last he was there, Elizabeth stirred in the bed, and when Bill took her hand, he immediately felt her respond with a weak squeeze. But it was enough.

She was going to be all right.

For Elizabeth, waking up was like trying to rise through a pool of molasses. Every muscle in her body felt exhausted, and even breathing seemed an almost impossible chore. Slowly, she began to come back to consciousness, and then, feeling Bill's hand in her own, she forced herself to open her eyes.

She was not in her bed.

Not in her home.

Then the nightmare began to come back to her.

"Megan," she whispered, straining to sit up, but barely managing to raise her head from the pillow.

"Megan's fine," Bill told her. "She and Mrs. Goodrich are out in the waiting room, and all Megan has is a little cut on her forehead."

"Thank God," Elizabeth sighed. She dropped her head back onto the pillow, and her left hand moved to touch her belly in the nearly unconscious gesture she'd developed during both of her pregnancies.

At the movement, fear lurched inside her.

Then it came back to her: the terrible flash of pain, the breaking of her water, and the first violent contractions of labor. Contractions so unbearably painful that they'd caused her to pass out.

"The baby," she whispered. Her gaze fastened on her husband's, and though Bill said nothing for a second or two, Elizabeth could read the truth in his eyes. "No." The word emerged as a despairing moan. "Oh, please, no. The baby can't be . . ." Her voice faded away as she found herself incapable of uttering the final, terrible word.

"Shhh," Bill whispered, holding a finger to her lips, then brushing a lock of hair away from her suddenly clammy forehead. "The important thing is that you're all right."

The important thing. The important thing . . .

The words ricocheted through Elizabeth's mind, leaving bruises everywhere they went.

. . . you're all right . . .

But she wasn't all right. How could she be all right if their baby—their son—was . . . was . . .

"I want to see him," she said, her hand tightening in Bill's. "Oh, God, please let me see him." Her voice started to break. "If I can see him, I can make him all right." She was sobbing now, and Bill moved from the chair to the bed, gathering her into his arms to hold her close and comfort her.

"It's all right, darling," he whispered. "It's not your fault. It's just something that happened. We knew it might happen. It was hard enough when you had Megan, and maybe we just shouldn't have tried again. But it's not your fault. Don't ever think it's your fault."

Elizabeth barely heard the words. "The case," she whispered. "I put the doll in the case, and it fell on her. My fault. My fault."

"It was an accident," Bill said. "It wasn't anybody's fault."

But Elizabeth still heard nothing of her husband's words. "I lifted it off her. I lifted it up so she could get out. And it killed our son. It killed our son. . . ." Her words dissolved into broken sobbing. For a long time Bill held her, stroking her hair, soothing and comforting her. Finally, after nearly half an hour, her sobbing began to ease, and the terrible convulsive shaking that had seized her slowly lost its grip. A little while later Bill heard her breathing drift into the long rhythmic pattern of sleep, and felt her body at last relax in his arms. Kissing her gently, he eased himself up from the bed, then tucked the sheet and blanket close around her. He kissed her once more, then quietly slipped out of the room.

The strange numbness had already begun to set in as he walked back down the corridor toward the waiting room.

His son—for indeed the baby had been a boy, just as he and Elizabeth had hoped—was dead.

Dead, without having ever taken a breath.

Should he ask to see the baby?

The thought alone made him wince, and instantly he knew he would not. Better to keep an image in his mind of what might have been: a happy, grinning, gurgling son for whom no dreams would be too great.

Better to cling to the memories of a future that might

have been than to gaze directly at the tragedy that had just befallen him.

To see the child who might have been would bring far more pain than Bill McGuire could bear, and in the days to come Elizabeth—and Megan too—were going to need everything he had to give.

He pushed through the doors to the waiting room, and it seemed to him that neither Megan nor Mrs. Goodrich had moved at all. The old housekeeper still held his daughter close, and though Megan's head rested against Mrs. Goodrich's ample bosom, her eyes were open and watchful.

Cradled in her arms, she held the doll.

For an instant, and only an instant, Bill was tempted to snatch the doll from Megan's arms, to tear it apart and hurl it out into the night, to destroy utterly the thing that had come into their house only this morning and already done such damage to their lives. But that thought, too, he discarded from his mind. The doll, after all, was not at fault, and Megan, at least, seemed to be taking a certain comfort from it.

Pulling a chair close to the sofa, he sat down and took his daughter's hands.

"Is he here?" the little girl asked. "Has my brother been born?"

Bill felt a sob rise in his throat, but determinedly put it down. "He's been born," he said quietly. "But he had to go away."

Megan seemed puzzled. "Go away?" she repeated. "Where?"

"To heaven," Bill said. A gasp of sorrow escaped from Mrs. Goodrich's throat. Her arm tightened around Megan, but she said nothing. "You see, Megan," Bill went on, "God loves little children very much, and sometimes He calls one of them to come and be with Him. Remember how He said, 'Suffer the little children to come unto me'? And that is where your brother's gone. To be with God."

"What about my Elizabeth?" Mrs. Goodrich whispered, her eyes wide with fear.

"She's going to be all right," Bill assured her. "She's asleep right now, but she's going to be just fine." He stood up. "Why don't I take you and Megan home?" he said. "Then I'll come back and stay with Elizabeth."

Mrs. Goodrich nodded and got stiffly to her feet. Her hand clutching Bill for support, she let him guide her out to the car. Megan followed behind them, the doll held tightly in her arms.

"It's all right," Megan whispered to the doll as they passed through the glass doors into the night. "You're better than any brother could be."

Chapter 7

*E*lizabeth McGuire stayed in the hospital for three days, and on the afternoon that Bill finally brought her home, the weather was every bit as bleak as her mood. A steel-gray sky hung low overhead, and the first true chill of winter was in the air. Elizabeth, though, hardly noticed the cold as she walked from the garage to the back door of the big house, for her body was almost as numb as her emotions.

The moment she entered the house, she sensed that something had changed, and though Bill suggested she go right up to their room and rest for a while, she refused, instead moving from room to room, unsure what she was looking for, but certain that she would know it when she found it. Each room she entered seemed exactly as it had been before. Every piece of furniture was in place. The pictures still hung in their accustomed spots. Even the mahogany case in the library was back where it belonged—screwed to the wall with much heavier hardware this time, so the accident could never be repeated—and even most of the objects it contained had been repaired and put neatly back in their places. Only the doll was gone. Elizabeth shuddered as she gazed up at the empty shelf where she'd placed it. Apart from the doll, all was as it should have been.

The photographs were back in their silver frames; the shattered glass all replaced.

Fleetingly, Elizabeth wondered if her spirit could be

repaired as easily as the damage to the pictures, but even as the question came to mind, so also did the answer.

The pictures might have been made right again; she would never be.

Finally she went upstairs, retreating wordlessly to her room.

Later that night, when Bill had come to bed, she remained silent. Though she could feel the warmth of his body lying next to hers, and his strong arms holding her, she still felt more alone than she ever had before. When finally he drifted into sleep, she lay awake gazing up at the shadows that stretched across the ceiling, and began to imagine them as black fingers reaching out to squeeze her sanity from her mind as her own body had squeezed her son from her womb. Elizabeth realized then that it wasn't the house that had changed. It was she who was different now. Long minutes ticked away the night while she wondered if she could ever be whole again.

Finally she left the bed, slipping out from beneath the comforter so quietly that Bill didn't stir at all. Clad only in her thin silk nightgown, but oblivious to the damp chill that had seeped into the room through the open window, she walked on bare feet through the bathroom that connected the master bedroom to the nursery next door. In the dim illumination from the street lamps outside, the bright patterned wallpaper had lost its color, and the animals that appeared to gambol playfully across the walls when she had hung the paper a few short months ago now seemed to Elizabeth to be stalking her in the night. In the crib, lying in wait on a satin comforter, lay a forlorn and lonely-looking teddy bear.

Alone in the darkness, Elizabeth silently began to weep.

"Maybe I should just stay home today," Bill suggested the next morning as the family was finishing breakfast.

Elizabeth, sitting across from him at one end of the huge dining table that could seat twenty people if the need should ever arise, shook her head. "I'll be fine," she insisted, though the pallor in her face and her trembling hands belied the words. "You have a lot to do. If I need anything, Mrs. Goodrich and Megan can take care of me. Can't you, darling?" she added, reaching out to put her arm around Megan, who was perched on the chair next to her.

The little girl bobbed her head. "I can take care of Mommy. Just like I can take care of Sam."

"Sam?" Bill asked.

"That's what I named my doll," Megan explained.

Bill frowned. "But Sam's a boy's name, honey."

Megan gave her father a look that declared she thought he was being deliberately dense. "It's short for Samantha," she informed him. "Everybody knows that."

"Except me," Bill said.

"That's because you're a boy, Daddy. Boys don't know anything at all!"

"Boys aren't so bad," Bill said quickly, his eyes flicking toward Elizabeth.

"I hate them," Megan declared. "I wish they were all d—"

"You wish they were all girls like you, right?" Bill interjected quickly, cutting off his daughter before she could quite finish the last word.

"That's not what I was going to say," Megan protested, but by now her father was on his feet and had come around the end of the table to lift her out of her chair.

He held her high up over his head.

"I don't care what you were going to say," he said, swinging her low, toward the floor, then lifting her up once again. "All I care about is that you take as good care of your mommy as you do of your dolly. Can you do that?" Megan, overcome by giggling, nodded, and Bill set her down on the floor. "Good. Now run along and let me talk to your mother for a minute." When she was gone, Bill dropped down next to Elizabeth. "You're sure you'll be all right?" he asked.

"I'll be fine," Elizabeth assured him. "You do what you have to do. Megan and Mrs. Goodrich will take care of me."

Rising from her chair, she walked with him to the door, kissed him good-bye, then stood watching until his car had disappeared around the corner. But when he was finally gone and she'd shut the door, she slumped against the wall for a moment, afraid she might collapse to the floor without its support. A moment later she heard Mrs. Goodrich behind her, clucking worriedly.

"Now you get yourself back upstairs and into bed, young lady," the housekeeper said, reverting to the same no-nonsense tone she'd used years ago, when she felt Elizabeth wasn't behaving in a manner she considered quite proper. "The best thing for you is a good long rest, and there's nothing in this house I can't take care of."

Too tired to do anything but agree with Mrs. Goodrich's command, Elizabeth mounted the stairs. But when she reached the door of the master bedroom, instead of going inside, she paused, gazing down the hall toward Megan's room, whose door stood slightly ajar. Though she heard no sound coming from her daughter's room, something seemed to be drawing her to it. A moment later she was standing in the doorway gazing at the doll, which sat on Megan's bed, propped up against the pillows.

It seemed to be gazing back at her. Something in its eyes—eyes that now seemed so lifelike she could hardly believe they were only glass set in a porcelain head—reached out to her, touched a nerve deep inside her, took hold of her. Elizabeth picked the doll up, cradled it in her arms, and walked slowly back to her own room, closing and locking the door behind her.

Sitting down in front of the mirror above her vanity table, she put the doll in her lap and began brushing its hair, humming softly. As the brush moved gently through the doll's hair in a soothing rhythm, the numbness within Elizabeth began to lift and the pain began to ease. When the brushing was finally done, Elizabeth moved to the chaise, stretching out on it, the doll resting on her breast, almost as if it were nursing. Warmed by the morning sun streaming though the window, and comforted by the doll resting against her chest, Elizabeth drifted into the first peaceful sleep she'd had since losing the baby.

Bill McGuire was starting to wonder if anything was ever going to go right again. Since the day Jules Hartwick had told him the Blackstone Center loan was on hold, it seemed as if everything that could go wrong, had. Worst of all, of course, had been Elizabeth's miscarriage. After Megan's birth they'd been told it was unlikely that Elizabeth would be able to conceive again, and they had all but given up hope of a second child when Elizabeth discovered back in April that she was pregnant. "But it's going to be tricky," Dr. Margolis told them. "And this will definitely be the last." So now it was over, and though Bill still felt a terrible sense of emptiness and loss, the agony of that first night when he'd come back to Blackstone to find that his son had been born dead had already begun to dull.

He knew he was going to survive it, and that somehow he would carry Elizabeth through the loss as well.

As if the loss of his son were not enough, it seemed the gods were somehow conspiring against him. He had raced home from Port Arbello thinking he'd won the condo project. But yesterday he'd received a call from the developer to tell him that the contract—the contract he'd counted on to carry him through until the Blackstone Center project came back to life—had gone to an outfit from Boston, which came in with a late bid that Bill knew he couldn't possibly undercut. In fact, he was certain the Boston firm had no intention of staying within the bid they'd submitted, and planned to make up their losses on change orders. He'd argued with the developer, but the man would not be convinced. So now he was back at the bank on the slim hope that Jules Hartwick might have some good news for him. As he pulled his car into a parking slot, however, he saw Ed Becker going into the bank. A preoccupied scowl on the lawyer's face was enough to tell him that whatever news might be coming out of Jules Hartwick's office would not be good.

Instead of entering the bank, Bill veered off the other way and walked down the street to the offices of the *Blackstone Chronicle*. An old-fashioned bell tinkled as he pushed the door open, and all three people in the office looked up.

Angela Corelli, the young woman who served as receptionist and secretary, and Lois Martin, who had been Oliver Metcalf's assistant editor and layout artist for fifteen years, greeted him with embarrassed smiles and quickly downcast eyes. Only Oliver immediately got up, came around from behind his desk, and took his hand. "I'm so sorry about what happened," he said. "I know how much you and Elizabeth were looking forward to the new baby."

"Thanks, Oliver," Bill said. "I'm just starting to think maybe I'm going to make it, but Elizabeth's taking it pretty hard."

The older of the two women in the office finally seemed to recover her wits. "I was thinking I should call her," Lois Martin offered. "But it's just so hard to know what to say."

"I'm sure she'd appreciate hearing from you," Bill told her. "But you might want to wait a couple of days."

"If there's anything any of us can do, just let us know," Oliver said. He gestured to the wooden chair in front of his desk. "Got time for a chat?"

"Actually, I was hoping I might be able to pick up some news," Bill said. "About the bank."

Oliver shrugged. "Your guess is as good as mine. I

keep calling Jules Hartwick, but I always get steered to Melissa Holloway instead."

Bill sighed. "Well, at least I no longer feel like I'm the only one. How can someone who looks that sweet be that efficient? And how'd she get to be second in command at her age?"

"Takes after her father," Oliver replied. "One of the smartest men I ever met, except when it came to picking a wife. Charles Holloway's a terrfic lawyer, but his second wife was a terror. Hated Melissa. Melissa got through it, though."

But Bill McGuire had stopped listening, his mind already focusing on what to do next, calculating how much money he had in the bank—assuming the bank wasn't about to collapse—and how long it would last him. The numbers gave him no comfort. The fact of the matter was that the odds of finding a construction job that could carry him through till spring were pretty much zip. If he was going to avoid going broke, he was going to have to get to work on a new line of credit. He rose to his feet. "If you hear anything—anything at all—let me know, okay?"

"You'll hear it before I even start to write the story," Oliver promised.

As they walked toward the front door, it opened and Rebecca Morrison stepped inside. Taking in the number of people in the little newspaper office, though, she blushed crimson and turned to leave again.

"Rebecca?" Oliver said. "What is it? Can I help you with something?"

She hesitated, then turned back, her cheeks still flushed red. Her eyes nervously flicked from one face to another, but finally came to rest on Oliver. Taking a tentative step toward him, she held out her hand. "Th-this is for you," she said. "Just because you're always so nice to me." Her flush deepening once again, she turned away and quickly ducked out the door.

Oliver peered into the bag. Inside, wrapped in shiny silver foil, were a dozen chocolate Kisses. When he looked up again, everyone in the office was staring at him.

Staring, and smiling.

Oliver broke into a smile too, wishing Rebecca hadn't scurried out of the office quite so fast.

"Well, at least some people's lives are going right," Bill McGuire said, slapping Oliver on the back as he left the office.

Seeing how happy the little bag of silver-wrapped chocolates had made Oliver, his own troubles no longer seemed quite so grim. Maybe, Bill thought, he'd just stop at the candy store and pick up a bag for Elizabeth. No, make that three bags; no sense in leaving Megan and Mrs. Goodrich out.

Suddenly, Bill McGuire felt better than he had in days.

An hour later Elizabeth came awake again, stretching languorously, savoring the feeling of well-being that had replaced the terrible torpor she'd felt earlier this morning. But as the last vestiges of sleep were sloughed away and she came back to consciousness, she slowly became aware of someone moving around in the next room.

The nursery.

Megan?

But what would Megan be doing in the nursery?

Rising from the chaise and carrying the doll with her, Elizabeth went through the bathroom and into the nursery.

Mrs. Goodrich, her back to Elizabeth, was in the process of emptying the contents of the little dresser, which stood against the opposite wall, into a large cardboard box.

"Who told you to do that?" Elizabeth demanded.

Startled by Elizabeth's words, Mrs. Goodrich whirled around. "Oh, dear," she said. "You frightened me, popping out of the bathroom that way. You go on back to bed, dear. I can take care of all this."

"All what?" Elizabeth asked, moving out of the bathroom doorway into the middle of the room. "What are you doing?"

Mrs. Goodrich placed the tiny sweater she held in her hands into the box and took another from the dresser drawer. "I just thought I'd get all this packed away for you, and put away in the attic."

"No," Elizabeth said.

Mrs. Goodrich blinked. "Beg pardon?"

Elizabeth's voice hardened. "I said no, Mrs. Goodrich." Her voice began to rise. "How dare you come in here and start packing all my baby's clothes."

"But I thought you'd want—" Ms. Goodrich began. Elizabeth didn't let her finish.

"I don't care what you thought. Go back downstairs and leave me alone. And from now on, stay out of this room!" Mrs. Goodrich hesitated, but before she could argue, Elizabeth spoke again. "Just go! I'll take care of this."

Mrs. Goodrich stared at Elizabeth in shock, barely able to believe her ears. Should she try to argue with her? she wondered.

No, she decided. Better not to say anything right now. After all, given what she'd been through, Elizabeth couldn't be expected to be herself quite yet. It was her own fault, really. She should have given Elizabeth more time before she began packing away the things in the nursery.

Laying the sweater in her hand on the top of the dresser, Mrs. Goodrich quietly left the room.

When she was gone, Elizabeth went to the dresser and began removing the clothes—the little play suits and pajamas, the tiny overalls, bibs, and shirts—from the box, carefully smoothing each one out and refolding it before putting each item back in the drawer from which it had come.

"How could she do that?" she asked the doll, which she'd sat on the dresser so it was leaning up against the wall, exactly as if it were watching what she was doing. "Doesn't she realize you're going to need all these things?" Taking a small sweater out of the box, she shook it out, then held it up against the doll. "Still a little big, but in a few months it will fit perfectly, won't it? What could she have been thinking of?" Still talking to the doll, Elizabeth folded the sweater and put it in the drawer next to the bottom, with all the other sweaters. When the box was empty and all the baby clothes were back where they belonged, she picked up the doll and carried it to the crib, where she carefully tucked it under the comforter and kissed it softly on the cheek.

"Time for a nap," she whispered. "But don't you worry. Mommy will be right here." Settling into the blue rocking chair next to the crib, Elizabeth softly began crooning a lullaby.

From the open doorway to the hall, unnoticed by her mother, Megan watched.

Chapter 8

"Something's wrong with Mommy," Megan announced as her father came through the front door. She was sitting on the bottom step of the hall stairway, her face stormy. "She took Sam."

"Your doll?" Bill asked. "Why would she do that?"

"I don't know," Megan replied. "And she got mad at Mrs. Goodrich too. Real mad." Then she saw the paper bags tied with red ribbon, and got up. "Is that for me?"

"One bag's for you," Bill told her, "and one's for your mother, and one's for Mrs. Goodrich." He gave her one of the little bags of chocolate Kisses. "You can have one now. Then we'll put the rest away for later."

"Mommy shouldn't get any," Megan said. "If I were bad, you wouldn't let me have any."

Bill knelt down so his eyes were level with his daughter's. "Honey, Mommy isn't being bad. She's just very, very sad right now. And if she took your doll, I'm sure there's a good reason."

Megan shook her head. "She just wanted it. But Sam wants to be with me."

"I'll tell you what," Bill said. "I'll go up and talk to Mommy, and see if I can find out why she took Sam. Okay?" Megan nodded, her hand disappearing into the bag, emerging with a fistful of Kisses. "Only one now," Bill said. "You can have another after lunch. And we'll save the rest for later."

Megan hesitated, calculating the odds of getting her

way if she begged for more of the candy right now. Reluctantly, she dropped all but one of the chocolates back in the bag. As her father started up the stairs, though, she quickly sneaked another one, and then a third.

Bill headed for the master bedroom, expecting to find Elizabeth either in bed or lying on the chaise. But the room was empty. Then, through the open door to the bathroom, he heard the soft creaking of the antique rocker in the nursery. Why would Elizabeth have gone in there? Since the miscarriage, even he hadn't been able to bring himself to go into the room they'd been preparing for the new baby. And for Elizabeth, going into the nursery had to be agonizing. Yet something had drawn her into it.

He crossed the bedroom and stepped into the connecting bathroom. Though the door opposite him stood ajar, he could see little of the room beyond. And now in addition to the creaking rocking chair, he could hear Elizabeth, quietly humming a lullaby.

He pushed the door to the nursery farther open.

Elizabeth was seated in the chair. Her back was to him, but he could see that she was holding something in her arms.

Something to which she was humming the quiet song.

"Elizabeth?" he asked, starting toward the chair.

The rocking stopped, as did Elizabeth's humming. "Bill?"

He bent over to kiss her on the cheek, but pulled back abruptly.

In her arms, wrapped in the soft pink and blue woolen blanket they had bought only a week earlier, was the doll. Its blue eyes were staring up at him, and for the tiniest fraction of a second Bill had the feeling that they were watching him. But then the moment passed and he brushed his lips against Elizabeth's cheek.

Her flesh felt oddly cold.

"Honey? Are you all right?"

Elizabeth nodded, but said nothing.

"I brought you something."

A flicker of interest came into her eyes, and she stood up. "Let me just put the baby back in his crib."

The baby . . . The words echoed in Bill's mind as Elizabeth gently laid the doll in the crib and tucked the little blanket around it. "How come you brought Megan's doll in here?" he asked as she turned back to face him. A flash of confusion appeared in Elizabeth's eyes, and then they cleared.

"Well, we don't really know the doll was meant for her, do we?" she asked, but there was a brittleness to her voice that sent a warning chill through her husband. "It could have been for the new baby, couldn't it?"

"I suppose it could," Bill conceded uneasily. "But don't you think—"

"Can't we just leave it here for now, at least?" Elizabeth pleaded. "When I came in here this morning, the room just seemed so empty, and lonely, but when I brought Sam in, it just seemed to fill right up." Her eyes flicked toward the crib. "Sam," she repeated. "What a nice name. I always thought if we had a boy, it would be nice to name him Sam."

Another warning current tingled through Bill. Though he and Elizabeth had discussed a lot of names, he couldn't remember either one of them ever mentioning Sam. "I think Megan really—" Bill began, only to be quickly interrupted by his wife.

"Megan can get along without the doll for now," she said. "And it will only be for a day or two." She smiled at him, then moved close, putting her arms around him. "I can't explain it, really," she whispered, her lips close to his ear. "It just makes it easier for me. Can't you understand that?"

Bill's arms closed around her and he wished there

were something—anything—he could do to ease her pain. "Of course I can understand," he replied. "If it makes you feel better, there's no reason you can't keep the doll in here for a little while. I'm sure Megan will understand."

In the hall outside the nursery, Megan scowled angrily. Her father hadn't taken the doll away from her mother after all.

In fact, he'd told her she could keep it.

And Megan didn't understand.

She didn't understand at all.

Chapter 9

*T*he moment Bill awakened, he knew Elizabeth was no longer beside him, but as the big clock downstairs began to strike midnight, he still reached out to his wife's empty place in the hope his instincts might have betrayed him.

They had not. The bed was empty, the sheets almost as cold as the room itself.

He lay in bed for a moment, trying to decide what to do. The evening had not been easy for any of them. First he'd had to try to explain to Megan that right now her mother needed the doll more than she did. "Mommy's sick," he'd told her. "And she needs the doll to take care of her."

"But she's always sick," Megan had protested. "And I need Sam to take care of me!"

"In a few days," he'd promised, but he could see the doubt in Megan's eyes, and when Elizabeth finally came down for supper, the three of them sat tensely at the table. Megan, usually full of chatter about what she'd been doing all day, barely spoke at all, and Elizabeth was utterly silent.

After dinner he'd tried to interest his wife and daughter in watching a videotape, but Megan quickly retreated to her room, and although Elizabeth sat beside him on the sofa in the library, he knew she wasn't paying attention to the movie. Finally, a little after nine, they both came up to bed.

While he stopped in to kiss Megan good night, Elizabeth went directly to their room. He told himself she'd sensed

Megan's anger and was simply giving her daughter some time to get over it, but deep inside he suspected that Elizabeth had simply not been able to consider Megan's feelings, any more than she'd been able to concentrate on the movie.

"Mommy doesn't love me anymore, does she?" Megan had asked when he'd gone in to say good night. Her voice was quavering, and though he couldn't see her face in the shadowy room, he'd tasted the saltiness of tears when he kissed her cheek.

"Of course she loves you," he'd assured her. "She's just not feeling well, that's all."

But Megan had not been consoled. "No, she doesn't," she insisted. "She just loves Sam."

He'd tried to assure her that things would be better tomorrow, when the two of them would go and find a Christmas tree, but even that hadn't cheered Megan up. When he left her room, she'd already rolled over, turning her back to him.

Things had been no better with Elizabeth. She was already in bed, and though he knew she wasn't asleep, she hadn't responded when he tried to cuddle her close to him. At last he'd given up, contenting himself with lying next to her and holding her hand, determined to stay awake until he heard her breath drift into the steady rhythms of sleep.

But he hadn't been able to stay awake, and now he'd awakened to find himself alone.

The last gong of the hour struck, leaving the house in silence. Then he heard the squeak of the rocking chair. Slipping out of bed and putting on the thick woolen robe Elizabeth had given him two Christmases ago, he went through the bathroom into the nursery.

Elizabeth was sitting in the rocking chair she had rescued from the attic and painted pale blue.

Once more, she was humming a soft lullaby to the doll, as she had when he'd come home in the afternoon.

But tonight she was doing something else as well.

The pale skin of her bare breast gleamed in the moonlight, and he could see the doll's head pressed firmly against her nipple.

He went to her and knelt beside the rocking chair. "Come back to bed, darling," he whispered. "You're so tired, and it's so late."

For a moment he wasn't sure she heard him, but then she turned her head and smiled at him. "In a minute," she said. "I have to finish feeding the baby, and then put him down for the night."

Though she'd spoken the words softly, in a voice so sweet it broke his heart, they still sliced through him like tiny knives.

"No, darling," he said. "It's not a baby. It's just a doll." He rose to his feet and reached down as if to take the doll from her, but she shrank away from him, and he saw her arms tighten. "Elizabeth, please," he said. "Don't do this. You know it's not a—"

"Don't say it!" she commanded, her voice rising. "Just go back to bed!"

"For God's sake, Elizabeth—" he began again, but once again his wife cut his words off.

"Leave me alone!" she shouted. "I didn't ask you to come in here! And I know what I'm doing! I can take care of my baby!" She was on her feet now, and there was a look in her eye that frightened Bill.

"It's all right," he said, forcing his voice back to a gently soothing tone. "Of course you know what you're doing, and of course you can take care of the baby. It's just late, that's all. I thought maybe I could help you."

"I can do it," Elizabeth said, her voice taking on an edge of desperation. "I can take care of my baby. I know I can. Just leave us alone and we'll be fine." Her eyes met his now, beseeching him. "Please? Can't you just leave us alone for a little while?"

Suddenly Bill felt utterly disoriented. Was his wife losing her mind? What should he do?

Take the doll away from her? No! That would only make things worse.

The doctor. He should call Dr. Margolis. Dr. Margolis would know what to do. "All right," he said, taking care to keep his voice perfectly level. "I'll go back to bed, and you take care of—" He faltered for a moment, but then managed to finish the sentence. "—the baby. And when he's gone to sleep, you'll come back to bed. All right?"

Elizabeth nodded, sinking back into the rocking chair. His throat constricting as a sob formed in his chest, Bill turned and hurried back through the bathroom, carefully closing the door behind him. But instead of going back to bed as he'd told Elizabeth he would, he went downstairs to the desk in the library, and the telephone.

After the twelfth ring he finally heard the sleepy, and faintly annoyed, voice of Dr. Margolis.

An hour later Elizabeth was back in bed, the pills the doctor had given her already taking effect. "I'll be all right," she said as she began to drift into sleep. "Really I will. All I need to do is take care of my baby and I'll be all right." Then, as Bill kissed her gently, her eyes closed.

Leaving Mrs. Goodrich to watch over Elizabeth, Bill led the doctor down to the library, where he poured each of them a shot of his best single-malt scotch. "I don't know about you, but I really need this," he said, handing Margolis one of the glasses, then draining half the other.

"I'm not sure it's as bad as you think it is," the doctor observed, taking a sip of the whiskey, rolling it around in his mouth, then swallowing it.

"For God's sake, Phil! She thought the doll was a baby. *Our* baby!"

The doctor's brows arched slightly. "She's had a terrible shock, Bill. I don't think any man can truly understand how hard it is for a woman to lose a baby.

Especially when she knows there's no chance of having another one, and she thought she was long past any danger."

"But to fantasize that a doll is—"

"But isn't that what little girls do all the time? Don't they pretend their dolls are real babies?"

"It's hardly the same thing."

"Isn't it?" Margolis countered. "Why not? The way I see it, Elizabeth is in so much pain right now that she simply can't deal with it. So tonight she projected all her maternal feelings—the ones she's been storing up, ready to shower on your son—onto the doll. I suspect it was far more an emotional release than a true delusion."

"And you don't think I should be worried?" Bill asked, hope mingling with his doubt.

"Of course you should be worried," the doctor replied. "Hell, if you weren't worried, I'd be more concerned about you than about Elizabeth. All I'm saying is that I think right now you need to cut Elizabeth a lot of slack. I suspect that by morning she'll be feeling a lot better. But even if she wants to pretend the doll is her baby for a day or two, where's the real harm? Right now she's got hormones raging through her, causing all kinds of confusion, and she's in just as much turmoil emotionally as she is chemically. Let's just give her another day to calm down, and then take another look at how she's doing. Deal?"

Bill hesitated, but as he turned Margolis's words over in his mind, he began to see their wisdom. Finally he took the doctor's outstretched hand. "Deal."

In her room, Megan lay in her bed, watching the shadows on the ceiling. She'd been awake a long time, listening through the nursery door, hearing every word her mother and father had said.

And now, as she lay gazing at the dark shapes above her, she heard another voice.

The voice of the doll.

But tonight it wasn't calling out to her.

Tonight it was whispering.

As it spoke, Megan listened, and began to understand what she must do.

Chapter 10

*T*he next morning dawned bright and clear, with no trace of the slate gray overcast that had gathered like a shroud over Blackstone nearly every day of the past week. Leaving Elizabeth to sleep as long as she could, Bill was dressed and at the desk in the library by six. By eight, when Megan came in to report that Mrs. Goodrich was going to throw his breakfast away if he didn't come to the table *right now,* he'd reached the conclusion that if he and Elizabeth were reasonably careful about what they spent, they might just make it through until Jules Hartwick's problem at the bank was cleared up. At the worst, only a small loan would be needed, and there was far more than enough value in the house to secure whatever loan might become necessary. Then, as he and Megan were finishing breakfast half an hour later, the phone rang and the need for a loan suddenly evaporated.

"I'm wondering if you might have any free time," Harvey Connally said. It was clear in the old man's voice that he was aware of the problems with Blackstone Center.

"Depending on the project, I might be able to work you in," Bill replied.

"I thought you might," Connally observed dryly. "Here's the deal. My nephew Oliver has been wanting to do some remodeling down at the *Chronicle.* Seems he's decided he needs a private office, and I thought it might make a nice Christmas present for him."

"It would make a nice Christmas present for me too," Bill said.

"Always like to spread the cheer around." Connally chuckled. "Hate to see anyone get their holidays ruined. Why don't you meet me down at Oliver's little place in about an hour?"

As Bill hung up the phone and went back to the dining room, the load of worries he'd been carrying for the last few days seemed just a little lighter.

Megan watched from the front porch until her father had disappeared down Amherst Street, then she went back into the house, closing the door silently behind her. In her mind she could still hear the doll whispering to her, just as it had last night.

"Go to the kitchen," the doll's voice instructed. *"See what Mrs. Goodrich is doing."*

Obeying the voice, Megan moved through the dining room and the little butler's pantry, and pushed open the kitchen door. Mrs. Goodrich was sitting at the table, mixing a large bowl of batter.

"No tasting," the old woman warned as Megan reached a finger into the bowl, scooping out a large dollop of dark brown dough studded with chocolate bits. "Well, maybe just one," the housekeeper amended as the lump of dough disappeared into the little girl's mouth. "But that's enough," she added, rapping Megan's knuckles lightly with a wooden spoon as she reached for a second helping. "Now, you just stay out of my way for half an hour, and then we'll start getting the Christmas things out. And this year you can set the crèche up on the mantel all by yourself."

Snatching one last morsel of the batter, Megan left the kitchen.

"Half an hour," the voice in her head said. *"That's a long time."*

As the voice whispered to her, Megan went upstairs

and paused outside her parents' bedroom. The door was closed, but when she pressed her eye to the keyhole, she could see that her mother was still in bed.

Megan waited, watching. After a full minute had passed, she decided that her mother was still asleep. Moving farther along the hall, she passed the door to the big linen closet, then went through the next one.

The nursery was filled with morning sunlight, and as Megan gazed around at the new wallpaper and all the new furniture her parents had bought for the baby, she wondered if maybe she shouldn't listen to the doll after all, if she should ignore the voice. But even as the thought came into her mind, she heard the voice whispering to her once again.

"This room is much nicer than your room," it said. *"They didn't buy you new furniture."*

Megan carefully closed the door, then crossed to the crib.

The doll lay beneath the pink and blue blanket. Its head was turned so that it seemed to be looking directly at her.

"Pick me up," the doll commanded.

Megan obeyed.

"Take me to the window."

Cradling the doll, Megan walked over to the window.

"Open the window."

Setting the doll down, Megan raised the window as high as she could. Then, still following the instructions being whispered in her head, she picked up the doll and crept out onto the roof that pitched steeply away from the gabled window. Holding on to the sill with one hand, she laid the doll as far from the window as she could.

The doll slid on the wet shingles of the roof. Megan's heart raced as it tumbled closer to the edge. Then its skirt caught on the rough edge of one of the shingles and it came to a stop six inches from the rain gutter and the straight drop to the flagstone terrace below.

Pulling herself back into the nursery, but leaving the window open, Megan ran through the bathroom and into her parents' room.

"Mommy!" she cried. "Mommy, wake up!" Rushing to the side of the bed, Megan began shaking her mother. "Mommy! Mommy!"

Elizabeth jerked awake, the voice of her baby still echoing in her ears. Even after she opened her eyes, the voice persisted. Finally, through the haze of sedatives, Elizabeth recognized it.

Megan.

"Honey?" she said, struggling to sit up as her daughter tugged at her. "What is it? What's wrong?"

"The baby," Megan told her. "Mommy, something's wrong with the baby. Come on!"

The baby! Then it hadn't just been a dream—her baby really had been calling to her. Throwing the covers back, Elizabeth climbed out of bed and stumbled through the bathroom to the nursery.

The crib was empty!

"Where is he?" Elizabeth cried, her voice rising as panic welled up in her. "What's happened to him?"

"He's outside, Mommy," Megan said, pointing to the open window. "I tried to stop him, but—"

Elizabeth was no longer listening. Rushing to the window, she peered out into the bright morning sunlight.

There, lying on the shingles only a few inches from the edge of the roof, was her baby. How had it happened? How had he gotten out there?

Her fault.

It was all her fault! She never should have left him alone. Never!

If he tried to turn over—tried to move at all—surely he'd fall.

Elizabeth leaned out the window, reaching as far as she could, but her baby was just beyond her reach. Gathering

her nightgown around her hips, she crept out onto the
steep roof, hanging on to the casement of the window.

"Help me," she told Megan. "Just hold on to my hand."
As Megan came close to the window and gripped her
mother's wrist in both her hands, Elizabeth released her
grip on the casement.

"Now," the voice whispered in Megan's head.

Obeying the voice without question, Megan let go of
her mother's wrist. Elizabeth began to slide, her bare feet
finding no purchase on the wet shingles. A second later
her right foot caught in the rain gutter. For an instant she
thought she was going to be all right. Reaching out, she
snatched up the doll, but it was already too late. Her
balance gone, and with nothing to catch herself on, Elizabeth pitched forward, plunging headfirst onto the flagstone terrace, the doll clutched protectively against her
breast.

Leaving the window wide open, Megan left the nursery,
made her way down the stairs, then ran through the living
room to the library. Unlocking one of the French doors,
she stepped out onto the terrace.

Her mother lay sprawled on her back, her head twisted
at a strange angle, blood oozing through her blond hair.

In her arms was the doll, still pressed protectively
against her breast. Squatting down, Megan carefully
pried her mother's hands loose from the doll, then
cradled it against her own chest.

"It's all right, Sam," she whispered to the doll as she
took it back into the house, quietly closing and relocking
the French door. "It's all right," she repeated as, without
so much as a glance back through the glass of the French
doors, she left the library and carried her doll back up to
her room. "You're mine now. Nobody's ever going to
take you away from me again."

Bill McGuire sensed nothing amiss when he came back
to the house an hour later. The sweet smell of chocolate

chip cookies was wafting from the back of the house; Mrs. Goodrich was taking the last batch out of the oven as he entered the kitchen.

"Well, isn't this good timing," the old woman said as Bill helped himself to one of the cookies that were piled high on a platter on the table. "I was just going to take some up to Miss Elizabeth, but I'm not really sure my old bones could get me up there."

"Don't even think about it," Bill told her. Putting half a dozen cookies on a smaller plate, he left the kitchen and went upstairs. As he was about to go into the room he and Elizabeth shared, though, he heard Megan singing softly.

Singing a lullaby.

Turning away from the master bedroom, he continued down the hall to his daughter's room. The door stood wide open, and Megan was lying on her bed, propped up against a pile of ruffled pillows.

In her arms she held the doll.

When she saw her father standing in the doorway, the lullaby she'd been singing faded into silence.

"I thought we decided Sam could stay in the nursery for a while," Bill said.

Megan smiled at him. "Mommy changed her mind," she said. "She gave Sam back to me."

"Are you sure?" Bill asked. "You didn't just take her out of the crib?"

Megan shook her head. "Mommy said she knows Sam isn't a real baby, and that she doesn't want her anymore. She told me to take good care of her and always love her."

As Bill listened to the words, a sense of uneasiness began to come over him. "Where is she?" he asked.

Megan shrugged. "I don't know. After she gave Sam back to me, she went back in the nursery and closed the door."

Bill's uneasiness turned to fear. Telling Megan to stay in her room until he came back, he went to the nursery.

Opening the door, he was greeted by a blast of cold air surging in through the open window.

The doors to both the bathroom and the master bedroom beyond stood wide open. "Elizabeth?" he called. "Elizabeth!"

Going to the window, he started to close it. Before he could pull it shut, however, his eyes fixed on the roof outside.

Some of the shingles appeared to be hanging loose.

As if something had disrupted them, and then—

"Elizabeth!" he shouted, then turned and ran from the room.

A few seconds later he was in the library, at the French doors. Through the windows, he saw his wife, and a moment later, as he cradled her lifeless body in his arms, a terrible howl of grief erupted from his throat.

Upstairs in her room, Megan smiled at her doll. And the doll, she was almost certain, smiled back at her.

Chapter 11

Bill McGuire was utterly unconscious of the icy chill in the air on the day he buried his wife, for he was far too numb to be aware of anything as insignificant as the weather. Bareheaded, he stood at the head of Elizabeth's grave. Megan was on one side of him, holding on to her father with her left hand as she clutched the doll in her right, pressing it against her breast almost as if to prevent it from seeing the coffin that stood only a few feet in front of them. On Bill's other side was Mrs. Goodrich, one of her hands tucked into the crook of his arm, her face covered by a thick veil. The old woman seemed to have shrunk since Elizabeth died three days earlier, and though she had continued to go through the motions of taking care of Bill and Megan, the spirit had gone out of her. Bill could not help thinking that the Christmas rapidly approaching would be her last.

Even the house seemed to have gone into mourning; a silence had descended over it, broken only by Megan, for whom, Bill suspected, the truth of what had happened had not yet sunk in. Each night, as he tucked her into bed, she looked up into his eyes and repeated the same words.

"Mommy's all right, isn't she?"

"Of course she is," Bill assured her. "She's with God, and God is taking care of her."

Last night, though, Megan had said something else: "Sam's sorry," she'd whispered.

"Sorry?" Bill had asked. "About what?"

"She's sorry Mommy had to go away."

Bill had assumed that, like so many children who lost a parent when they were very young, Megan was afraid that somehow she might have been the cause of her mother's death. But the thoughts were far too painful to face directly, so she was projecting them onto the doll. "You tell Sam not to worry," he told her. "What happened to Mommy wasn't Sam's fault, or your fault, or anyone else's. It was just something that happens sometimes, and all of us must try to help each other get through it."

But how was Megan going to help him get through it? How was he ever going to be able to forgive himself for leaving Elizabeth alone that morning? How must she have felt when she awakened?

Alone.

Grieving.

Bereft.

And remembering what had happened the night before, when she'd thought the doll was her baby. What must have gone through her mind? Had she thought she was going insane? Was she afraid she was going to end up like her sister, confined for the rest of her life in a sanitarium? And he hadn't even been there to comfort her.

Surely he could have put Harvey Connally off for a few hours.

But he hadn't, and for that he would never forgive himself.

Bill heard Lucas Iverson begin the final prayer, and as Elizabeth's coffin began to descend slowly into the grave, Bill closed his eyes, unable to watch these final moments. When Rev. Iverson fell silent once again, Bill stooped down and picked up a clod of soil. Holding it over the coffin, he squeezed his fingers and the lump broke apart, dropping into the open grave.

The same way his life was breaking apart and falling away.

His eyes glazing with tears, he stepped back from the grave's edge and stood silently as one by one his friends and neighbors filed past to pay their last respects to Elizabeth, and offer their condolences to him.

Jules and Madeline Hartwick had come, along with their daughter and her fiancé. The banker paused, laying a gentle hand on Bill's shoulder. "It's hard, Bill. I know how you feel."

But how could Jules know how he felt? he wondered. It wasn't his wife who had died.

Ed Becker was there too, with Bonnie and their daughter, Amy, who was only a year younger than Megan. While Bonnie Becker murmured sympathetic words to him, he heard Amy speaking to Megan.

"What's your dolly's name?"

"Sam," he heard Megan reply. "And she's not a little boy. She's a little girl, just like me."

"Can I hold her?" Amy asked.

Megan shook her head. "She's mine."

Bill knelt down. "It's all right, honey," he said. "You can let Amy hold Sam."

Again Megan shook her head, clutching the doll even tighter. Bill looked helplessly up at Bonnie Becker.

"You can hold her another time," the lawyer's wife said quickly, taking Amy by the hand. "Just tell Megan how sorry you are about her mother, and then we'll go home. All right?"

Amy's large dark eyes fixed on Megan's. "I'm sorry about your mother," she said.

This time Megan made no reply at all.

Rebecca Morrison, accompanied by her aunt, Martha Ward, was next. As Martha stood glaring at her niece, Rebecca struggled to speak, her eyes downcast in shy embarrassment.

"Thank you for coming, Rebecca," Bill said, taking her hands in both his own.

"Tell him what you wanted to say, Rebecca," Martha Ward urged her niece, causing Rebecca's face to flush.

"I—I'm just so sorry—" Rebecca began, but her voice quickly trailed off as the words she and her aunt had rehearsed vanished from her memory.

"We're so terribly sorry about poor Elizabeth," Martha said, her eyes flicking toward her niece in disapproval. "It's always such a tragedy when something like this happens. Elizabeth was never a very strong woman, was she? I always think—"

"Elizabeth bore more in her life than most of us have ever been asked to," Bill cut in, his eyes fixed on Martha Ward. "We'll all miss her a great deal." He put just enough emphasis on the word "all" to throw Martha off her stride. Then, seeing how mortified Rebecca was by what her aunt had said, he managed to give her a friendly hug before turning to the next people in line.

The faces began to run together after a while. By the time Germaine Wagner approached, pushing her mother in a wheelchair, he barely recognized them. When Clara Wagner informed him in a stern voice that he "must come for dinner one night," he had no idea how to respond. He knew Germaine from the library, of course, but had never been inside the Wagners' house, and certainly had no desire to go there now.

"Thank you," he managed to say, then turned quickly to Oliver Metcalf and Harvey Connally.

"Watch out for that one," Connally warned dryly, watching Germaine push her mother away. "As far as she's concerned, you've become fair game."

"Jesus, Uncle Harvey!" Oliver Metcalf protested. "I'm sure Mrs. Wagner didn't mean anything like—"

"Of course she did," the old man cut in. "And don't tell me I'm saying something inappropriate, Oliver. I'm eighty-three years old, and I shall say what I please." But as he turned back to Bill McGuire, his tone softened. "It's a terrible thing you're going through, Bill, and there's nothing any of us can say that's going to make it easier. But if there's anything I can do, you tell me, understand?"

Bill nodded. "Thanks, Mr. Connally," he said. "I just keep wondering if maybe—" The words died on his lips as he felt Megan slip her hand into his.

"Don't think that way," Harvey Connally advised. "Things happen, and there's no explaining them, and no changing them. All any of us can do is play the hand we're dealt, the best way we can."

Ten minutes later, when the little cemetery was empty save for the three of them, Harvey Connally's words still echoed in Bill McGuire's mind.

Play the hand we're dealt, the best way we can.

Gazing one last time at his wife's coffin, Bill McGuire finally turned away from the grave and started out of the cemetery.

Mrs. Goodrich, leaning slightly forward, dropped a single rose onto the coffin, then reached down to take Megan's hand.

But Megan lingered for a moment, and though she still faced the coffin, her eyes were fixed on the doll.

The doll gazed back at her.

Now they truly belonged to each other, and no one would ever take the doll away from her again.

Late that night, as Blackstone slept, the dark figure moved once more through the silent corridors of the abandoned Asylum, at last coming again to the room in which the secret trove of treasures was stored.

Glittering eyes flicked from one souvenir to another, and finally came to rest on a single sparkling object.

A hand, smoothly gloved, reached out and picked up a locket, holding it high so it glimmered silver in the moonlight.

It would make a perfect gift.

And the dark figure already knew who its recipient would be.

To be continued . . .

*The serial thriller continues next
month . . .*

JOHN SAUL'S
THE BLACKSTONE CHRONICLES:
Part Two
Twist of Fate: The Locket

As plans to demolish the old Blackstone Asylum
have been delayed, the people of the town begin
to feel the cold chill of terror and foreboding. For
somewhere deep behind the eerie stone facade
that once housed madness, a mysterious hand
selects another gift: a silver locket. Which
member of the community will feel its evil
power? Will it be Jules Hartwick, the bank president . . . Oliver Metcalf, the editor of the local
paper . . . the lovely library assistant, Rebecca
Morrison . . . or some other unlucky soul?

Only time will tell. . . .

To be continued . . .

THE PRESENCE
by John Saul

In all his bone-chilling novels, *New York Times* bestselling author John Saul has proved himself an architect of pure terror and psychological suspense. Now get ready for his most frightening novel yet—a story ripped from the blackest part of night. There is something evil in the air—but how can you hope to run from something you can't even see?

BEWARE
THE PRESENCE

Coming in Summer 1997
A Fawcett Columbine Hardcover Book

JOIN THE CLUB!

Readers of John Saul now can join the John Saul Fan Club by writing to the address below. Members receive an autographed photo of John, newsletters, and advance information about forthcoming publications. Please send your name and address to:

The John Saul Fan Club
P.O. Box 17035
Seattle, Washington 98107

Be sure to visit John Saul at his Web site!
www.johnsaul.com

Visit the town of Blackstone on the Web!
www.randomhouse.com/blackstone
Preview next month's book, talk with other readers, and test your wits against our quizzes to win Blackstone prizes!

TRUE TERROR

ONLY FROM

JOHN SAUL